"This Book Belongs To.
Amy Basinger

JOHNNY REB

JOHNNY REB

By

MERRITT PARMELEE ALLEN

DECORATIONS

by

RALPH RAY, JR.

DAVID McKAY COMPANY, INC.

New York

JOHNNY REB

LIBRARY OF CONGRESS CATALOG CARD NUMBER 52-5635

JOHNNY REB

Chapter 1

THERE was a great noise in the woods, a crashing and thrashing in the underbrush, the muffled pounding of horses' hoofs and the voices of excited hounds on a hot trail. The stream of sound flowed down a brush-cluttered gully toward a rocky ridge that blocked its farther end with ranks of terraced ledges against which the approaching clamor beat itself into echo fragments.

Above the gully, on the left side, two panting boys parted the bushes and looked down in time to see a large black bear lope silently across the clearing and out of sight.

"Goner!" grunted the larger boy, man-size in stature, throwing back his long black hair angrily.

" 'Tain't our bear anyway," the other said. He was contrastingly slight, blond and quick. "The Hamptons put him up."

"Think the Hamptons own the wild critters?"

"It's fair to let anybody finish a hunt he's started, Bert."

"Yeh! I'll show you what I think uv Hamptons."

Bert raised his shotgun, loaded with buckshot, as a black-and-tan hound tore into the clearing, bugling open-mouthed on the nose-high scent. The younger boy's right foot went up, kicking the muzzle of the gun into the air a split second before it went off.

"Damn you, Ez, I'll kill you fer that!" Bert spun around.

"No, you won't." The smaller boy looked him in the eye. "Why won't I?"

" 'Cause you won't, that's why. You should be 'shamed, aiming to shoot a neighbor's dog."

"Them puffed-up, high-nosed Hamptons hain't no neighbors uv mine."

"Oh, shut up," Ezra said wearily. "I've heard that blab till I'm sick of it."

"Pa says—"

"I don't care what he says! Shut up! Here come the Hamptons. Mister, they can ride!"

A powerful brown horse crashed into view, heavy as a draft animal but light on his feet, a hunter of fine breeding. He was ridden by a giant who sat superbly, and they were followed by two younger men on equally good mounts. Three flashes and they were across the clearing and into the woods again.

The boy named Ezra followed without a look behind to see if his companion were coming. He was a fast runner and parted the bushes with both hands, for he carried no gun, making almost as good time as the horsemen. It was a short race, for when the bear came to the first ledge across the head of the gully he wheeled to fight the hounds. Rearing up, back to the rocks, mighty paws ready with extended claws, foam dripping from his savage open mouth, he waited. The dogs pranced in front of him, whining and barking, the younger ones scratching at outcroppings of rock in their eagerness to get behind him. The horsemen pulled up at about ten yards and sat watching the play for a minute. Ezra knew them to be Wade Hampton and his sons, Wade and Preston, and he ran faster, for he knew what to expect.

He was not disappointed. The man flipped his bridle rein to young Wade and swung to the ground, lightly for all his great size. Whipping a long double-edged knife from a sheath that hung on his belt, he ordered the dogs back and walked toward the bear. It would be a primitive fight but a fair one, one big animal against another, each relying on skill and physical strength. Hampton respected bears and scorned as unsportsmanlike the use of firearms against them.

The bear roared, perhaps contemptuously, when he saw he was opposed only by a man on foot. It would be easy. He swayed on his great pads and waited, savage claws hooked and ready. Hampton walked carefully, glancing from the bear to the ground to make sure of his footing. The two boys sat their horses tensely, each with a hand on his pistol. Behind them Ezra stood on tiptoe, his mouth open and dry with excitement. His eyes were on Hampton who had at that moment touched the spring that lies deep in every boy's heart and released a flood of hero worship.

The bear struck first, reaching like lightning with his right paw. Hampton was quicker, and so perfect was his judgment that the claws swept between his neck and the point of his right shoulder. The bear swung again, a cuffing blow with his left paw that would have felled a horse. Hampton ducked and, as the great black arm swished over his head, leaving the heart unguarded for a moment, he drove the long knife in up to the hilt, yanking it out as he stepped aside.

The bear roared horribly and came down on all four feet,

then reared again when he saw the man still facing him. Blood gushed from his chest, mouth and nose, but he fought heroically. To whimper and run was not in his code. A beast, yes, but full of the courage a man might envy. Hampton watched for his chance and, when it came, drove the knife into the throbbing throat. The breath whistled from the severed windpipe; the bear clutched his chest as a man might have done, sank on his haunches, swayed and fell over on his side.

"Brave fellow!" Hampton said in a deep voice, as he pulled a handful of leaves and wiped his knife.

The two boys stood in their stirrups and cheered, though Preston's face was white.

"How many does that make, Father?" he shouted, to relieve his feelings by speech, for he knew the score.

"Eighty-four—two for each year of my life."

"By 1900, another forty years, there won't be any bears left." Young Wade laughed.

"Don't, Wade!" Preston said quickly. "We don't want him to go on risking his neck."

"Father will never meet his match, Pres."

"He may," Preston answered, half to himself.

While they were talking, Ezra had slipped through the bushes to examine the dead bear. The excitement of the fight had made him bold beyond custom. But the bear was not dead; with a last spasm of life he flicked out a paw and ripped the boy's right leg from knee to ankle. Wade shouted, but Preston, who was his father's double, pulled a pistol and shot the animal through the head.

Ezra did not make a sound, but he leaped back and fell from fright. The pain had not begun. Hampton, who could throw the carcass of a four-hundred-pound bear across a horse's back, picked him up like a straw tick and sat him down with his back against the ledge.

"Easy, lad," he said gently. "You're not badly clawed."

"Don't mind me." Ezra tried to sound casual, but his mouth twisted as fire seemed to shoot up his leg. "It was my fault; I had no business messing with your bear."

"Close your eyes while I examine it," Hampton said in a matter-of-fact tone. "It will be bloody at first. Tie the horses, Wade, and make a tourniquet from your handkerchief. Take my hat, Preston, and fetch it full of water from the brook."

The boys answered, "Yes, sir," and obeyed instantly, like soldiers.

Hampton cut off the trouser leg and tossed it against a rock, where it landed with a sodden thud and slid slowly to the ground, leaving a trail like a splash of red paint. He watched the throbbing wound for a moment, then motioned Wade for the tourniquet, which he put in place and twisted tight with a stick. Preston, still white-faced, came with the big felt hat full of water. His father nodded, soaked a handkerchief in it, and began washing away the blood.

"Does it hurt like the Old Harry?" Preston whispered, bathing Ezra's face with his own water-soaked handkerchief.

"No," the boy lied, opening his eyes and smiling wanly.

Preston liked him for that. The freckle-faced lad might be of little account in the neighborhood according to social standards, but he was no crybaby.

"Father is almost as good as a surgeon," he said reassuringly. "He is always patching us up. You just trust him."

"I do," Ezra said truthfully.

He did not close his eyes again, but sat watching the senior Hampton's face. It was the face of an aristocrat. A thick dark beard covered most of it, and a sweeping mustache seemed to support the long straight nose. The eyes counted most, bright blue eyes, large and thoughtful and piercing. They were eyes that, if Ezra did not miss his guess, could blaze like lightning. They were the kind of eyes that fitted such a bold, ruddy, weather-beaten countenance, yet they went well with the high broad forehead and the crest of wavy brown hair.

To Ezra, as to many people in South Carolina, Wade Hampton was part of a tradition. He was a great man descended from others of the same name, a politician, a scholar, a planter wealthy enough to own three thousand slaves, but, for all that, the best horseman, shot and athlete in all the South. Heretofore he had been an unapproachable figure to the "poor white" boy, a figure on horseback, or a speechmaker at the state capital in Columbia, yet here he was, down on his knees, doing all he could to help a poor boy who had blundered into his bear hunt and been hurt. He wasn't as big as God—the preachers said nobody was anywhere near that size —but they must have a lot in common.

"You are a lucky boy." Hampton finally sat back on his heels and smiled with his eyes. "None of the large blood vessels are injured. The bleeding will soon stop."

"Thank you," Ezra replied and, remembering how the boys addressed their father, added, "sir."

"Wade," Hampton said, "you are the only one wearing a clean linen shirt—rip it up for bandages."

"Yes, sir, of course." Wade pulled off his coat.

"Don't do that!" Ezra shook his head.

"Why not?" Wade smiled.

"I'll be all right. Don't waste a shirt." Ezra had never owned a linen shirt and the thought of deliberately tearing one to pieces shocked him.

"This is an old one." Wade pulled it off.

"I believe you are Ezra Todd?" Hampton asked.

"Yes, sir."

"Well, Ezra, I want to take you home with me until your leg heals. As your physician, I have a professional interest in your case." He smiled again.

Perhaps he knew, though there was nothing he said to suggest it, that the shanty where Ezra lived with old Jed and Bert was too filthy a place to be laid up in. But the mere thought of going inside the mansion at *Sand Hills* scared the boy.

"I couldn't do that, sir," he said, trying to sound polite but firm. "Jed wouldn't like me to."

Hampton took a bandage from Wade. As he began wrapping it on the leg, he inquired carelessly, "He is neither your relative nor legal guardian?"

"No, sir, but I sort of must do as he says."

"How old are you, Ezra?"

" 'Most seventeen."

"You do not refuse to come home with me so I may keep an eye on that leg for a few days? You will be doing me a personal favor."

Jeepers! The great Wade Hampton putting it that way to a boy from down the creek! Refuse that man anything? No sir-ee!

"I'll go with you, sir."

"Thank you, Ezra." Hampton tied the bandage and began wrapping another.

Ezra closed his eyes, not because of the pain, but because he felt weak at the sudden turn of events. To be yanked out of Jed Sears' shack and treated as an equal by the Hamptons, though only for a few days, was enough to make a fellow feel dizzy.

"Shall we start now?" Hampton's voice brought him to himself.

"Any time, sir."

A powerful hand gripped his and raised him to his feet. A ton of pain seemed to be tugging at his right leg and Ezra gasped in spite of himself.

"You will ride Preston's horse," Hampton said.

"Can he carry both of us?" Ezra moved his leg a little, cautiously.

"He can, but I am not too frail to walk two miles," Preston laughed. He was handsome and almost as tall as his father, for all he was only eighteen.

"I won't make you all this bother," Ezra protested.

"Nonsense!" Preston snorted and went to get his horse.

They helped the lad mount and steadied him when they saw him turn white with pain.

"Whar you goin'?" It was Bert's voice.

Ezra saw the big fellow standing at the edge of the bushes, his heavy mouth open as it always was when he was angry.

"I am going home with Mr. Hampton," the boy answered

"No, you hain't."

"The bear clawed me, Bert. Mr. Hampton is doctoring me."

"Us Searses takes keer uv our kinfolkses," Bert snapped.

The way he said it was a deliberate affront to Ezra's new friends and the boy shot back, "I'm no kin of the Searses and you know it."

"Git offen thet hoss."

"I won't for you."

"Wait till I tell Pa."

"Tell him and be cussed to you!"

"Perhaps I can explain the situation," Hampton put in blandly. "Inasmuch as it was my bear that injured Ezra, I judge it only fair that I repair the damage as far as possible."

"*Yore* b'ar!" Bert growled. "Thet thar's *my* b'ar. I jumped him 'n' was follerin' him when you cut in."

"That's a lie!" Ezra cried.

"Shet yore mouth!" Bert roared. "Didn't you hear me shoot?" he demanded of Hampton.

"I heard a shot."

"He shot at your hounds—or tried to," Ezra said, trembling with anger.

"I'll kill you fer thet!" Bert shouted.

"So I've heard before."

"Shamin' yore folkses by suckin' round quality!"

Ezra wondered why one of the boys didn't knock Bert down, but the young Hamptons only seemed amused by his ranting.

" 'N' I tell you, mister, I want thet b'ar," Bert went on.

"Take it," Hampton said calmly. "But, understand, it is a gift, not a tribute, from me." He dismissed the whole matter by adding to Preston, "Please lead Ezra's horse, son, and we will follow."

"I'll pull you offen thet hoss, Ez," Bert threatened.

Preston's blue eyes snapped as he remarked quietly, "I wouldn't do that if I were you."

Bert did not move, but, as he watched them enter the woods, he yelled, "You hain't seed the last uv me!" Which, unfortunately, was true.

Chapter 2

THAT ride of little more than a mile was a journey between two worlds to Ezra Todd. The wonder of it possessed his mind and kept his thoughts in such a whirl that he
almost forgot the pain in his leg. The fact that the Hamptons
were handsome, wealthy and cultured was enough to make
people like Jed and Bert hate them. The Searses had tried to
make Ezra share their hatred and, though he had never done
so, he had taken it for granted that the owners of *Sand Hills*
were snobs. Perhaps the folks, who didn't know that Good
Samaritan the preacher talked about, the neighbors, who just
saw Hampton ride by in the road and knew he was rich,
called him a snob too. Misunderstanding made an awful lot
of trouble, the way sand did in axle grease, and the hub and
the axle would keep on scratching each other as long as it was
there.

Preston led the big hunter to the main road, where Hampton and young Wade pulled out and cantered away.

"They are in a hurry to change," Preston explained. "The
governor and his staff are coming out from Columbia for
dinner."

Instantly Ezra found fear riding with him.

"I can't go home with you," he said, tightening the reins,
"not in these clothes."

"Poot!" Preston said, without slackening his stride.

"I'm all dirt and blood and rags."

"Two poots!"

"Besides, I don't know my manners with such folks."

"With your injury you won't be expected to meet the guests."

"Please, Mr. Hampton, let me get off and I'll walk home."

Preston stopped and turned around. "In the first place, Father said to bring you in, and what he says goes."

"I'm thankful for all he's done for me, but—"

"In the second place, you aren't able to walk home. And in the third place, you couldn't protect yourself if you got there. That big oaf threatened to kill you."

"Bert is all wind," Ezra explained.

"Is he your half brother?"

"No, not him!"

"For all that, in your condition you are taking no chances with the bully." Preston resumed leading the horse down the road.

"But," Ezra protested, "what'll the—the Governor of South Carolina say if he sees you bringing home a scarecrow like me?"

"We don't ask permission of the governor or anyone else to invite guests to our house." Preston answered in a tone that put an end to that part of the conversation. "Besides," he added, "he wouldn't notice you anyway. He only thinks of war."

"War with the North?" Ezra asked innocently.

"Naturally. What other war would he be interested in?"

"I don't know."

"Good lord! Don't you read the papers?"

"No."

"What!"

"Jed and Bert can't read and they're mad if I do."

"Do you mean to tell me you don't know what that Abraham Lincoln is up to, and what the South proposes to do about it?"

"I've heard it talked the South might pull out of the Union."

"That is exactly what we will do if those penny-pinching, double-dealing Yankees try to browbeat us." Preston's neck burned red under its tan.

"I've heard your father don't favor it," Ezra ventured.

"Father is a peace-loving man, if that's what you mean, but when the trumpets sound he will be the first to don his armor and ride forth to crush the barbarians who asperse the honor of our fair land." Preston saw nothing vainglorious in such a speech. Every educated young Southerner worshipped Sir Walter Scott and tried to emulate his heroes.

"You reckon there'll be a real war?"

"I hope so."

"You want to take a hand in it?"

"What absurd questions you ask! Don't you want to strike a blow for the glorious South?"

"I ain't thought much about it," Ezra answered honestly.

"I have, and I want to get in early before it is over. It won't last long. We can whip the Yankees in three months."

"There must be a lot of 'em to whip," Ezra remarked.

"Yes, but one of us is worth ten of them in battle."

"I wonder," Ezra said with provoking honesty.

"Are you a Yankee?" Preston spun around so quickly that the horse threw up its head.

"Why"—Ezra was puzzled—"I never thought I was anything but a United Stateser."

"You had better decide," Preston said gruffly and resumed walking. "This is no time to be on the fence."

Ezra felt uncomfortable. He didn't want to be rude, yet he had no definite idea about the war question because he knew nothing about it. He had gathered, of course, that there was friction between the North and South over slavery and what people called "States Rights," but it had little meaning for him. At most, it was something for politicians to chew on, and politicians, so Jed said, were all thieves and cutthroats. Ezra had never met one until two hours before, but he was ready to bet his head Wade Hampton was nothing of the kind.

"I reckon," he decided aloud, for Preston's benefit, "that till I know more about it I'll take your father's word for it. If I've got to git down off the fence, as you say, I'll come down on the South side."

"You are a prize!" Preston threw back his head and laughed. "Honestly, Ezra, you are so green that you are refreshing."

"I know I'm green," Ezra said with unexpected intensity. "I've been raised in the mud and I'm sick of it. I've got an awful hankering to git out in the sun and ripen off."

"By Jove!" Preston said impulsively. "I hope you do."

They were approaching the house at *Sand Hills,* and as

they turned in to the avenue Ezra looked about with uneasy wonder. It was the first time he had been nearer the place than the road, and to find himself passing among the lawns and shade trees and flower beds gave him the feeling that he was violating a privacy that was almost sacred. When they swung around the curved drive and pulled up at the broad steps, the white-pillared mansion with its two-story piazza gleamed like the Pearly Gates he had heard about. He would not have been greatly surprised to see seven-foot angels issue forth from it, with folded wings and twanging harps.

What did come out was a little old Negro, bearing an immense load of dignity under his white suit, and followed by a younger and larger one who radiated hospitality as though he owned the place.

"Hannibal," Preston said, "this friend has suffered a hunting accident. He is staying with us to recuperate."

If the butler wondered, as he must have, how a friend of the Hamptons happened to be wearing ragged jeans and a tow shirt, he betrayed himself by not so much as a flickering eyebrow.

"Yas, suh, Marse Presson," he agreed. "We got a room all ready fo' de gen'man to start recoupin'. Jeems, wipe that cat's grin offen yo' fat face an' assist de gen'man to dismount hisse'f."

"Oh me, oh my!" Jeems, now in the limelight, gestured tragically. "Is that pore laig busted, suh?"

"No, only scratched a little," Ezra told him. "I don't need any help."

"Yas, suh." Jeems reached up and almost picked the boy

out of the saddle. "Iffen Ah don' help a laig in dat fix, ma conscience am jes' one pain."

"All right." Ezra glanced up the steps and was thankful to see no one watching. The governor himself might have been there, or even a king or two, in this place. "I'll lean on your arm."

"Yas, suh. H'ist that laig easy so hit won't dissolve."

They went up with a fair degree of grace and speed and entered a great hall that glittered with mirrors and polished furniture. What kind of grease did they use to make the chairs shine so? Ezra wondered. And those stairs! Jeepers, they twisted upward like a hopvine on a pole. In a nearby room he heard voices and a woman's laughter.

"Come on, Jeems," he whispered in fright. "Get me out of here before they see me."

"Yas, suh." Jeems put a hand under his arm. "But a house guest don' haf ter hide hisse'f."

"I bet you never saw a house guest that looked like I do."

"How de ole b'ar look?" Jeems chuckled.

"Worse. Mr. Hampton killed him."

"Oh me, oh my! That man kills b'ars lak some folkses kill flies."

They gained the upper hall and went along it to a door with a crystal knob. Inside, the walls were covered with flowered paper, the first Ezra had ever seen, and the bed and chairs were dressed up in fancy cloth that was prettier than calico.

"Yo' jes' mak youse'f to home hyar," Jeems said graciously.

"Make myself to home here!" Ezra looked around. "Lord, boy, I don't dare sit down."

"Ah'll fotch yo' a bath," Jeems suggested pointedly.

"Fotch me a bath?" Ezra had always bathed in the creek.

"Sho. Yo' set, suh."

"Well—all right." Ezra rested gingerly on the edge of a chair and Jeems went out.

Quality folks all of a sudden! Ezra rubbed his sore leg and knew by the feeling he was not dreaming. Yet it was more like a dream, to start out with Bert at noon and wind up a few hours later in the Hampton mansion, with a boy waiting on him hand and foot. When he got home Jed would be fighting mad, for Jed hated anyone who was wealthier or more intelligent than he was, a fact that automatically kept him a-bristle against most of the world. Bert was the same way. Neither would ever be happy unless some calamity reduced all their neighbors to their own level. They believed in equality, providing that meant pulling others down instead of raising themselves up. Ezra chuckled. Mister, would they be hopping when they knew he had been hobnobbing with the Hamptons!

Two small boys entered, lugging a huge tub of hot water, followed by Jeems with an armful of towels, soap and clean clothing.

"Specs yo' want help, suh," he suggested.

"Of course not," Ezra said shortly, though he was wondering about the proper procedure. "Get along out now."

When the door closed behind them, Ezra picked up the clothes which he guessed had belonged to Preston at an earlier day. Then he pulled off his own, rags by comparison, and started to wash his face. Heck! The water smelled like the wild roses growing by the pasture fence—or it might be the soap. He squeezed the cake experimentally and it shot out of his hand under the bed. Painfully he retrieved it and, glancing in a long mirror, laughed aloud to see himself stalking a cake of soap as a cat would a robin. After that he handled the soap as though it were a wet fish and it gave him no more trouble, though he disliked the sissy perfume. He was willing to bet that Wade Hampton and his husky sons scorned the stuff—no sweet-as-a-rose fluff for them.

Judging from the towels, the bath was more or less a success. The clothes fitted at least comfortably, but he hesitated a long while before he put on the dressing gown. It was too much like a dress to suit his taste, but he finally argued himself into it with thoughts that, inasmuch as he could not pull a trouser leg over the bandages, he might wear the thing with honor. Yet when he saw himself in the mirror, he felt like someone's sister. He hoped the house would not catch fire so he would be obliged to appear in public. When a tapping sounded on the door he glanced instinctively at the bed, tempted to crawl under it.

"Who is it?" he asked, pulling himself together.

"Jeems, suh. Is yo' done finish yo' abolutions?"

"If you mean bath, yes."

"Yas, suh." The door opened and Jeems stepped inside, throwing his arms wide and nearly upsetting the two little Negroes behind him. "Oh me, oh my! Ain' that de mos' beautiful gown!"

"Do you like it on me?" Ezra grinned.

"Uh-huh! Yo' looks lak one dem young gen'mans from de Sout' Ca'lina College."

"Thank you."

The dream continued, while Ezra wondered what they would find to do for him next. One of the boys brought him a glass of light wine, while the other came with a newspaper; he tried to read it and got little sense from the pages, because it was all politics and talk of war. Then all three of his servants came in with something far more interesting: supper, with enough food and dishes and knives and forks and spoons and cloths to load a mule.

"Dis de fuss co'se," Jeems said gravely.

Ezra motioned the boys out of the room and then turned to Jeems.

"Look here, there's no use pretending," he said frankly. "I'm from down the creek and I don't know as much about this stuff as a frog. If I have to eat downstairs sometime, I'll act like a fool. Do you know what to do with all these tools?"

"Yas, suh, I'se a waiter at big doin's."

"Good! Will you stay here and tell me how to eat like a gentleman?"

"Yas, suh." Jeems took it as an honor, very seriously. "Yo' *am* a gen'man, suh."

"No, I'm not."

"Suh, de man who *ain'* a gen'man am jes' de one who try to mak' de servants think he am. Yo' *am*."

"Well, that's one way to look at it." Ezra laughed and felt better. "I'm hungry. Start the first lesson."

When the meal was finished Ezra had eaten more varieties of food than he knew existed and, what was more valuable, had acquired a substantial knowledge of table etiquette. He was by no means perfect, but he had the essentials to practice with if he got a chance. He didn't know why he wanted to learn these things, except that they were a part of the new world he was glimpsing. He had never heard of inherent tastes or of dormant qualities that might lie buried like seeds until, when conditions were favorable, they pushed up to the surface. He felt only that he wanted to know more about life beyond his horizon.

Later that evening Hampton came up to Ezra's room with a Dr. Taylor who was a guest at the party downstairs.

"How about it, Watt?" Hampton inquired, after the leg had been examined.

"A few stitches might help, but I think the wounds will heal as they are." The doctor started wrapping a fresh bandage. "A nice job you did, Wade. Been taking lessons?"

"Oh, long ago. It is a handy thing to know."

"Especially in the days ahead, eh?"

"I hope you are wrong, Watt, before God I hope so."

"But you know I am not."

"No one knows yet—no one knows yet." Hampton walked up and down the room and Ezra noticed how tired his eyes looked.

"There you are, my lad." Dr. Taylor's manner changed abruptly as he snapped shut his ointment box. "You should sleep like a lamb tonight."

"If you don't, this may help you to pass the time." Hampton pulled a book from one of his deep pockets and laid it on the table. "Good night, Ezra."

When he was alone Ezra picked up the book. It was *Ivanhoe*. He began to read, and for the second time that day a new world opened before him.

Chapter 3

EARLY the next morning the Hampton boys dropped into Ezra's room to say good-by before returning to South Carolina College. They were plainly excited about something, the nature of which Preston revealed when he danced across the room and sang out, "It's coming, it's coming, it's coming! The South's pulling out of the Union. If the Yankees don't like it, let 'em try to stop us, my lads."

"You are jumping the gun," Wade said soberly. "Father is still fighting hard to block secession."

"He can't do it," Preston said flatly.

"He is working on a speech now, to be delivered in the legislature tomorrow."

"Oh, I know he hates war, but when it comes he will be in it with every ounce of his two hundred and forty pounds." Preston laughed proudly, for his father was his idol.

"So will we all," Wade said. "What about you, Ez?"

"I told your brother yesterday I'm on the South side."

"That's the ticket!"

Both boys shook hands with Ezra and hurried away. When the sound of their horses died away down the road the house seemed empty. Ezra picked up *Ivanhoe* and resumed reading, as fascinated as he had been from the beginning. It was the first real book he had ever tackled. To find that he understood it and was able to reconstruct the scenes from print was as though he had tried his wings and found that he could fly. If all books were like that, how wonderful it would be to go on and on from one to another, opening new doors and looking at strange sights that were never twice alike! And no matter how much you took from a book, even if you absorbed all of it, there was just as much left in it for the next reader. It was money you could spend any number of times and still have.

When Jeems brought his breakfast they had another lesson in table manners.

"De pore laig still mizzable?" Jeems inquired.

"Much better." Ezra thrust it out. "I must be going home. Where can I find Mr. Hampton?"

"In de study writin' a big speech. But, suh—" Jeems shook his head—"de Angil Gab'iel don' dass disturb him."

"I don't want to disturb him."

"Miss Mary say if yo' kin walk hit mought pleasure yo'se'f ter go downstairs."

"All right, let's go." Ezra picked up *Ivanhoe*.

"Ah fotch de book, suh?"

"No, I'll carry it. I'm no invalid."

"Skuze me, suh, no gen'man lug truck iffen he trus' de boy."

"You mean if I carry the book it will look as though I don't trust you with it?"

"Yas, suh."

"Heck, take it then." Ezra limped from the room.

At the foot of the stairs he was met by Mary Hampton, the most beautiful woman he had ever seen, who looked not much older than her two stepsons.

"I am so glad you are able to be about again!" She held out her hand, giving him a smile that would have ripened a green persimmon.

"Thank you, ma'am." In awful panic Ezra realized he was wearing that sissy dressing gown. "I—I—" He stopped, blushing.

"Yes?"

"I ought to ask your pardon for being—for not being dressed up right."

"You look perfectly right," she said, sensing his misery.

"That robe mak' him look lak ole king Sollymun hisse'f," Jeems put in loyally.

"Much better, I am sure." Mrs. Hampton laughed. "Solomon never wore a robe that was made in London. Come into the library, Ezra." She opened a door.

"Whew!" He forgot the robe as he stared into the room. "Why, ma'am, there must be hundreds of books there."

"About ten thousand."

"Ten thousand books!"

She smiled slightly. "Grandfather Hampton began the collection. This sword here"—she turned to a great curved blade on the wall—"is the one he carried in the Revolution and in the War of 1812."

She moved about softly, for the floor was covered with a carpet as thick as moss, showing him the family portraits and talking until he felt at ease in the room. Then she left him and he sat by a window from which he could see a dozen slaves working about the lawns and gardens. They were plump and well-clothed, happy beyond doubt, not the kind of field hands he had seen on the small plantations along the creek. He wondered if these people wanted to be free, free to worry about bills and taxes and where the next meal was coming from. Such questions were making a lot of talk in the world, but they were beyond him. He shrugged, picked up *Ivanhoe* again and forgot the things of the present.

He read quietly for a while, then suddenly doubled over the book and gripped it with both hands. "Jeepers!" he burst out. "They've got him."

"They always do in stories."

"Oh!" Ezra looked up and went red, for Hampton stood there, laughter in his eyes. "I was reading about Cedric. I didn't know I talked out loud."

"How do you like the story, Ezra?"

"It's a whizzer, sir."

"Yes, Scott is good. How is the leg this morning?"

"A lot better. I can go home now well as not."

"Let me see it. Put it up on this stool."

Hampton sat on a chair and began removing the bandages. Ezra noticed that his usually ruddy face was almost gray, but his hands were steady. The man whose words echoed through the whole South and beyond was not too busy to help an unimportant boy.

"Where did you learn to read, Ezra?" he asked as he worked.

"From my folks."

"Then Jed Sears isn't your kin?"

"No, sir. My folks were Northerners. They said everybody up there goes to school."

"That is one advantage of Puritanism," Hampton remarked. "All of that belief must be able to read the Bible themselves."

"My mother had a Bible," Ezra said. "Jed burned it after she died. He hates books because he can't read."

"Your parents came South to live?"

"Yes, sir. Father had a lung disease. The doctor said he should go to a warm country. When I was ten years old he and my mother died of the fever."

"And then?" Hampton was replacing the bandages gently.

"Jed's wife took care of them. She was a good woman. I had no folks so she kept me. She died two years afterward. I stayed with Jed and Bert. I could work and there was no place else for me to stay."

"That is your home now?"

"It's where I stay—for a while yet."

"I see." Hampton stood up. He was so well-proportioned that his immense size did not seem unusual. "Your leg is much improved, but I want you to stay here for a few days and let Jeems look after you. I am going away."

"Oh," Ezra said politely.

Hampton walked to a window and, as he looked out at the gentle landscape, his powerful hands twisted the back of a chair until its joints cracked.

"There is going to be a war, Ezra," he said, in a voice the boy never forgot. "I hate it— O God, how I hate it! I have fought it with all I have, but the hotheads on both sides will not listen to reason." He walked about the room, looking at the books and pictures as though seeking help from them.

"I suppose Abe Lincoln is to blame," Ezra finally said, try-ing to sound like a man of the world.

"No more than you are," Hampton answered unexpect-edly. "Mr. Lincoln is the victim of a force he neither created nor accelerated. He is now trying to direct that force in what he believes to be the right direction."

"But I have heard, sir—"

"Yes, I know. There must be a scapegoat. But, Ezra—" Hampton spoke as gravely as though addressing the legisla-ture—"the true instigators of this war are those greedy men who long ago brought the first Negro slaves to this country."

Ezra stared in amazement, for Hampton owned thousands of slaves.

"Slavery is a curse; in principle I hate it," the big man went on, his thoughts far from the listening boy. "So many others feel the same way that the Negroes will eventually be free, whoever wins this struggle."

"Then why have a war?" Ezra asked innocently.

"To establish the right of secession which the North denies us."

"Oh," was all Ezra said, for he was ignorant of such things.

Hampton continued to explain to the boy. "Being free men, we claim the right to choose our form of government. The North says we must accept its form. We will not be coerced into abandoning the principle we hold sacred. Seces-sion, not slavery, is the issue."

"And the North don't like the—the secession idea, sir?" Ezra wished the conversation would turn to something he understood.

"Oh, no!" Hampton smiled faintly. "They call it wicked rebellion. Well, so was the American Revolution. Furthermore, the very states that now condemn us most were once on the verge of secession."

"Oh," Ezra said again.

"Look there." Hampton pointed to the portrait of an impressive-looking gentleman in military uniform. "He was my father. In the War of 1812 he was an officer on Andrew Jackson's staff and carried the news of the victory at New Orleans to Washington. That intelligence broke up the Hartford Convention of New England States which was assembled to consider seceding from the Union. So you see, lad—"

"Wade," Mrs. Hampton called from the hall, "a messenger has come from Columbia."

"Thank you, my dear." Hampton took a long step toward her, then stopped and looked down at the boy. "May I have *Ivanhoe*?"

"Of course, sir." Ezra handed him the book.

Hampton carried it to a writing desk that was built into a bookcase, uncorked an ink bottle and made a few quick strokes with a pen.

"Let it dry before you close it." He handed the open book to Ezra.

Across the flyleaf he had written: *To Ezra Todd from Wade Hampton*. And below it: *Fortes fortuna juvat*.

"That is Latin," he said. "It means fortune favors the brave. Good-by, lad."

He was out of the room and off—to war.

Chapter 4

THROUGHOUT the rest of the day there was a strange uneasiness at *Sand Hills.* The house servants moved about on tiptoe, and, when Ezra hobbled outdoors in the afternoon, he saw the gardeners and stableboys gathered in knots, rolling their eyes and gesticulating to each other. The slave quarters, which was a small village in itself, could be seen wearing a half-jittery, half-prayerful air as though preparing for a thunderstorm.

"What's up, Jeems?" Ezra asked that evening when the boy came to dress his leg.

"Wah done bus' out, suh." In his excitement Jeems spread ointment on his own nose instead of on the bandage.

"War has busted out where?"

"Yonder." Jeems pointed through the window with one hand while he rubbed his nose with the other.

"But where?"

"Oh me, oh my! How kin Ah know, suh? One nigger say he hear de gen'man from C'lumbia say 'twuz Cha'ston. Our mens is shootin' cannons dar."

"Who are 'our men'?"

"Good lawd, suh, us Souddeners. Yo' don' 'spect us am *Yankees!*"

"I don't know which side you folks are on."

"Iffen that ain' de foolishest notion—beg yo' pahdon, suh."

Jeems rubbed his nose briskly with a bandage, making it shine like a button. "Us am on Marse Hamp'on's side."

"But the Yankees want you to be free."

"What bizzness dat of de Yankees? Iffen dey stick dair nose inter our bizzness dey gwinter breed a scab onter hit."

"Do you all feel that way?"

" 'Cept a few cacklehaids."

When Ezra went down to breakfast he found Mrs. Hampton dressed for traveling. She looked as though she had not slept, but she told him quietly that Fort Sumter in Charleston Harbor had been fired upon by shore batteries and the war was on. She added proudly that William Preston, a relative, had fired one of the first guns. Now she was off to Columbia to join her husband and see what a woman could do to help.

"Can I do anything?" Ezra asked. "You see, ma'am, I'm so ignorant I don't know what war means."

"None of us knows—yet."

"Preston said it won't last long."

"I am sure it won't." She was very young and confident.

"Thank you, ma'am, for all that's been done for me here."

"It was nothing. When the war is over you and Mr. Hampton will hunt bears again, with happier results, let us hope." She smiled at him and hurried away.

That afternoon Ezra went home, for he would not accept more hospitality when the family was not there. Jeems would have given him a complete wardrobe of Preston's outgrown clothing with a trunk to carry it in, but he took only a necessary pair of trousers and wrapped the remnant of his old ones around *Ivanhoe*. A boy drove him down the creek road and pulled up at the Sears' shack with as much of a flourish as though it were a mansion.

Bert stood in the doorway, his heavy mouth open, and when he saw who it was he raised his head and bawled, "Pa! Pa, come see the quality folkses, quick!"

Jed Sears appeared, a long, lopsided man, with straw-colored hair and beard and watery blue eyes. He was always leaning against something, if nothing more than a berry bush, and he now fitted one shoulder to the doorframe before he remarked, "Hain't we puttin' on airs though! Hoss 'n' kerridge 'n' nigger driver when we don't own a hull shirt."

Ezra got down slowly and took his bundle.

"Thank you for bringing me down, Eph," he said to the boy.

"Yas, suh. Want Ah should he'p yo' inter de house?"

Before Ezra could answer, Bert roared, "No, he don't! Git outen here, y'u damn Hampton nigger."

"Run along, Eph," Ezra said softly. "You're a good driver. Some day you'll be a coachman."

"T'ank yo', suh." Eph grinned and drove away without a second glance at the others.

Ezra turned around and his face was white.

"Why can't you be decent to people, Bert?" His voice trembled with anger.

"People!" Bert scowled. "Since when wuz niggers people?"

"Yas." Jed stepped onto the ground and leaned against the shack. "Whar's yore manners, Ez, to say 'Thank you' to a nigger?"

"I say it to anybody who does me a favor."

"Mighty high soundin' sence you sucked 'round the Hamptons," Bert sneered.

"Yas," Jed added. "You shouldn't have went to *Sand Hills*, Ez. You know I hate them Hamptons."

"And I know why you hate 'em—because they're better than you are."

"Who say they're better'n I be?" Jed roared.

"You know they are."

"Wade Hampton's grandpappy was a pore man same's I be."

"And because he didn't stay so you hate the whole family."

"You're a sassy puppy, Ez."

"Want I should wallop him, Pa?" Bert offered.

"Naw, he's got a sore laig."

"Nary mind." Bert grinned smugly. "I got the b'ar. I bluffed ole Hampton inter givin' it ter me."

"Bluffed him!" Ezra snorted.

"I got the b'ar, didn't I?"

"Yes, but you didn't fool Mr. Hampton. He's a man who'd rather walk round a skunk than stir him up."

"I'll kill you iffen you sass me!" Bert shouted.

"Shet up," Jed drawled. "What you got thar, Ez?" He pointed at the bundle.

"My old pants. I can't wear 'em till I sew 'em up."

Ezra limped into the shack. How he hated the place with its filth, its few pieces of crude furniture and its mud fireplace! It had sheltered him for years, but he had worked his way and owed the owner nothing. That gave him a feeling of independence that he secretly cherished. He sat on his pole bed, with a pretense of resting his leg, and slipped *Ivanhoe* between the blanket and the cornhusk tick before the others followed him inside.

He was rubbing his leg when Jed entered, and he looked up to ask, "Did you know the war has started?"

"Heerd so this mornin'." Jed sank upon a stool and leaned against the wall.

"What do you think about it?"

"Don't know, don't keer. Let 'em fight. They kin afford hit, I cain't."

"They goin' ter hire folkses ter fight fer 'em?" Bert asked from the doorway.

"Shore, iffen any fightin' is did." Jed stuffed a chew of tobacco through the curtain of his drooping mustache. "Rich men don't fight."

"I'll bet they will," Ezra disagreed.

"Safer ter hire it did." Jed spat into the fireplace.

"Which side'll pay the mostest?" Bert asked with interest.

"Dunno. Aim ter hire out, son?"

"Shootin' fer pay don't sound so bad."

"It's just plain murder the way you look at it," Ezra declared.

"What else is thar ter fight fer 'ceptin' money?" Bert wanted to know.

"Loyalty," Ezra answered.

"What you mean by that?"

"Why, either to help your country or your friends," Ezra answered, thinking of the Hamptons and Ivanhoe.

"I fight fer who pays mostest," Bert declared.

"I don't fight fer nobody." Jed spat again. "I don't git myself shot up fer no rich men No'th ner South."

"What you goin' to do, Ez?" Bert asked, in a baiting tone.

"Mend my pants," Ezra answered curtly.

For the next three weeks he lived a triple existence. His leg healed fast and, as he worked in the patches of corn and potatoes with Jed and Bert, his thoughts were at *Sand Hills* or in old England. They were fighting thoughts, for his heroes were fighting men. Life seemed to be that way; you had to fight for something if you were to get anywhere. Wade Hampton knew it, much as he loved peace, or he would never have written in the book *Fortes fortuna juvat*. Ezra repeated the words and their English equivalent, "Fortune favors the brave," until when he closed his eyes he saw them burning like fire across the blackness.

Gradually the book, the only book he had ever owned, and the man who gave it to him merged, and he saw Hampton, wearing armor, galloping north to break lances with Abe Lincoln. He knew it was a senseless picture, but it persisted. And so did the question: What of the war? The few people he met, all of Jed's type, neither knew nor cared. To them it was something as far away as the moon and much less important, for they believed the moon influenced the growth of crops and the way fish bit. Ezra wanted to go to *Sand Hills* and inquire but he lacked the courage, for even though he was known there he could not walk up to the door and ask questions. He might have gone on to Columbia, but that was out of bounds as Jed would never allow the boys in town unless he was with them. So he worked and thought and, when the others were at a safe distance, pulled out *Ivanhoe* and reveled in its magic.

One afternoon in early May, Jed and Bert went fishing. They fished often and caught little because they were too lazy to tend their lines. Ezra was left to finish the potato field, which he did early by letting out a link; then he hung his hoe on the limb of a tree and hurried back to the book. In the story he had reached the trial of Rebecca and it held him breathless. He read slowly from lack of practice, but the meaning was clear—they would kill her by slow torture unless a champion showed up to fight for her. Jeepers! They must be a cheap bunch of yellow-bellies to stand around and let an innocent woman be handled that way. What had become of the Black Knight and Ivanhoe? Holy smoke, boys, knock out those buzzards before it is too late!

Ezra sat on his bed, doubled over the book, oblivious of everything except what it was telling him.

"So thet's how you hoe 'taters!"

Jed's voice blasted him out of the realm of Richard the Lion Heart. Ezra felt cold with fear, then hot with anger.

"I finished 'em," he said.

"What you got thar?"

"A book."

"Whar'd you git hit?"

"Mr. Hampton gave it to me."

"Is thet so! Baitin' you to read so's you won't earn yore keep. Give me thet book."

"I won't." Ezra looked him in the eye. "My name is written in it and it belongs to me."

"You sassy puppy! I'll break ever' bone in yore body!" Jed lunged across the room.

To save his neck Ezra dropped the book and ducked toward the door, but Bert stood there grinning, so he grabbed the poker and backed into a corner. Jed, an inherent coward, hesitated to press him. Instead, he picked up the book and tossed it to Bert.

"Take keer uv hit, son," he said, with a meaning wink.

"I won't let nothin' happen to hit, Pa."

Bert ripped the covers off with one twist of his powerful hands, then pulled the pages apart, tore them crosswise, and threw handfuls of paper over his head, laughing loudly.

Then it happened. Years of pent-up hatred exploded in Ezra's brain and, for the moment, he was wild enough to kill. He leaped across the room, snatched the shotgun from over the fireplace and fired point-blank at the open door where Bert had been standing. But Bert had thrown himself backward and outside. Ezra clubbed the gun and turned on Jed who let out a yell and moved fast, for once in his life, into the yard. Ezra reloaded and stood on the steps. Whether he were right or wrong there was a thrill in being master of the situation. The Searses had stopped running when they reached the road and now faced him, safely out of range.

"I'll have the law on you fer this!" Jed roared, shaking both fists. "We're goin' ter fetch the sheriff."

" 'N' he'll put you whar you won't feel so smart!" Bert screamed. "You cain't rough us 'n' git away with hit. We'll fix you!"

"Git!" Ezra shouted and fired just to show what he thought of them.

They ran down the road and Ezra stood there, wondering what to do next.

Chapter 5

EZRA knew one thing was certain. He could not stay there. Whether or not the Searses carried out their threat to have the law on him, he was through with this place forever. Henceforth he would be on his own, alone in a world that had never been too friendly toward him. His tangible resources were practically nothing: the clothes he stood in, an extra shirt and pair of jeans, a jackknife.

Even *Ivanhoe* was gone. He looked at the littered pages and his anger boiled again. Then his jaw set grimly; they had destroyed his book but they could never deprive him of the pleasure it had given him, nor could they quench the desire it had created in him to know more about the world. Some day, by the great horn spoon, he would have dozens of books of his own that he could read when and where he chose, outside the mean, narrow, little sphere of Jed and Bert.

Ezra looked down at the fragments of *Ivanhoe* strewn about like the broken body of a friend, and tears smarted in his eyes. He searched until he found the half page Hampton had inscribed, which he folded and put in his pocket, then he gathered the other pieces and burned them in the fireplace. It was the nearest thing to a decent burial he could give the book, putting it forever beyond the reach of further desecration. Then he rolled his spare clothes into a bundle and put some corn bread in his pocket. A look outside showed him no sign of his enemies, so he returned the shotgun to its place, closed the door, and walked unhurriedly toward the woods. He did not glance back, for he never wanted to see the place again. He was off to test the truth of those words, *Fortes fortuna juvat.*

The next morning he was on the streets of Columbia, free for the first time to look about as he chose. The state capital was in high spirits, people laughing and carriages and horsemen clattering briskly up and down. A red-and-blue uniformed band swung by, playing *The Girl I Left Behind Me* in a way that made the boy hold his head high and march with it for several blocks. It finally entered a building where some kind of meeting was being held and he sat on a box in front of a store to watch what might come along next. The sight of so many people moving about almost made him dizzy, for he was unaccustomed to seeing more than two or three in a whole day. Where were they all going and how could they make their way in and out without getting tangled up?

"Boy," piped a falsetto voice behind him, "how old would you say I am?"

He turned around and saw a very old gentleman with a gold-headed cane in one hand and a copy of the Charleston *Courier* in the other.

"Well, sir—" Ezra hesitated.

"Be honest, boy," the gentleman said earnestly. He was neatly dressed in black and his eyes shone sharply above his white beard. "Your answer may be very influential. What do you say my age is?"

"About ninety, sir."

"The devil!" The gentleman thumped the sidewalk with his cane. "Two devils—even three. If I look that old to you I would look much the same to a recruiting officer. They wouldn't take me. As a matter of fact, boy, I am ninety-four."

"Whew!"

"Blast the years, boy! Because I have survived a certain number of them I must turn a deaf ear—though I am not deaf at all—to Wade Hampton's call for volunteers. The devil—a dozen devils! I served with Wade Hampton's father and grandfather against the British and now—*now*, when young Wade asks help to whip the piddling Yankees, I must sit in a corner. The devil!" The old gentleman snorted through his aristocratic nose.

"Did you say, sir, Mr. Hampton wants men for to be soldiers?" Ezra was on his feet.

"Certainly he does. Don't you read the papers?"

"Not very often."

"The devil! Look here." The old gentleman fumbled with his newspaper, talking all the while. "Governor Pickens is a fool in most respects, but he had sense enough to commission Wade a colonel and give him authority to raise his own command. Here it is." He nodded at the paper. "Wade advertises for a thousand men—six companies of infantry, four troops of cavalry and a battery. And I must ignore the call! What wouldn't I give to be seventy again!" He snorted once more and started away.

"Just a minute, sir!" Ezra caught up with him. "Can you tell me where I can find Mr. Hampton?"

"Colonel Hampton he is, boy."

"Yes, sir. Where is he now?"

"With his regiment, of course. Would you expect to find Wade Hampton at a tea party in wartime?"

"No, sir. But I don't know where his regiment is."

"Go down this street till you come to open country. You will see his tents."

"Thank you, sir." Ezra dropped back.

"Hey, boy!" The old gentleman turned. "Are you going to enlist?"

"I'm going to try to, sir."

"God bless you!" He put out a long, blue-veined hand. "Shake hands with one who wishes you well."

"Thank you, sir." Ezra squeezed the old soldier's hand, then watched him march away, erect but obliged to use his cane.

Ezra had no trouble finding the camp of Hampton's Legion, as it was already named. It was the pride of the town and crowds of sight-seers flocked around the rows of trim new tents as if it were a carnival. A troop of cavalry trotted past— the first soldiers Ezra had ever seen—and his heart pounded as he watched them. Every man rode as though born to the saddle. They were superbly mounted and their spotless uniforms made him blink: rich gray breeches with gold-braided seams tucked into high boots, snug-fitting gray jackets with more braid and brass buttons, shining kepis set at a cocky angle. Mister, the boy thought, I would rather be a private in that outfit than a general anywhere else.

He walked up to a snappy-looking trooper who was standing guard over a pile of supplies and nodded in a friendly manner. The soldier looked through him and gave no sign of seeing him.

"Excuse me," Ezra said. "Can you tell me where I can find Colonel Hampton?"

The trooper did not bat an eye. Ezra waited a moment and then said aloud, but as though talking to himself, "Maybe he's deaf in that ear. I'll try the other one." He moved along a step and repeated the question.

"No," the sentry snapped.

"He ain't in camp?" Ezra persisted.

"Certainly. But he is too busy to give time to you."

"I don't aim to pester him," Ezra explained. "I want to enlist."

The trooper, who was really very handsome, took a long look at the dirty, ragged youngster, and said coldly, "You are wasting your time here. Hampton's Legion is an elite corps, composed entirely of gentlemen."

"You mean," Ezra asked, "to get into it a man must have money?"

"More than money—he must be a gentleman."

"Which I ain't?"

"Obviously not."

"That being the case," Ezra retorted smoothly, "you won't be surprised when I tell you to go straight to hell." He walked away.

Ezra moved to one side of the parade ground and sat under a tree. The place was humming with activity; baggage wagons rolled by with supplies, horsemen cantered back and forth on official errands and, farther away, companies of horse and foot were drilling. They might be soldiers but they acted more like schoolboys on a lark who were trying to take life seriously from a sense of duty, not because they felt that way.

Ezra pulled a spear of grass and chewed it thoughtfully. So you must be a gentleman to get into this army? Just what was a gentleman? On the outside, he used good English, had nice manners, dressed stylishly, and kept away from manual work. Did those accomplishments make a soldier? From what Ezra had heard, common everyday men had played a considerable part in fighting the British and the Indians in the old days. Inside, a gentleman was supposed to be very brave and honorable. But so were other people. And he must belong to a "first family," members of which called it "first" because it included themselves. Yes, but that explained nothing to the boy.

He got up and wandered about uneasily, wondering where his next meal was coming from in this strange world where a fellow couldn't help fight a war unless he had a record of parties and dances. He stopped to watch a dozen young soldiers who were coming up the field, obviously just released from drill and cutting up like boys out of school. As they divided to pass a mud puddle in the road Preston Hampton stepped out of a nearby tent. He was wearing a beautifully tailored new gray uniform and yellow gauntlets. Gee, Ezra thought admiringly, there is a gentleman!

The boys saw Preston and stopped in their tracks. Some shaded their eyes with their hands as though dazzled, others pretended to faint, and one threw up his hands and shouted, "I surrender!"

"Come out of those gloves, Pres," a big fellow ordered. "Come on out now. We can see you in there."

"And look at that uniform, boys!"

"Easy. Don't venture more than one eye at a time."

"That's not a uniform—it's a creation."

As they ribbed him they closed in, but warily, for though Preston was smiling he was on guard. He started to take off his gloves, which was a mistake, because the instant his hands were busy the crowd rushed him. He was a powerful boy and knew how to handle himself, but the odds of twelve to one were too much. They got him down, caught him by his arms and legs and ran to the mud puddle, where they dunked him thoroughly.

For good measure the big soldier was plastering his hair with mud, when Ezra hit him like a battering-ram and knocked him into the puddle beside Preston. The boy kept going and lashed out at the next man, who was so surprised that he took a blow on the chin that staggered him. Ezra tried to strike again, but his arms were caught and held by a dozen hands.

"What's this, a Yankee?" someone asked in a good-natured tone.

"A wildcat," another answered.

"Git up, Preston," Ezra shouted as he struggled and kicked. "We can lick 'em together."

Preston stood up and looked down in amazement at the wild-eyed prisoner.

"I'll be hanged!" he burst out. "It is Ezra Todd. What are you trying to do, Ez?"

"Ain't you going to fight?" Ezra panted.

"This is no fight," Preston explained. "It is my initiation."

"Your what?"

"I have just been made a lieutenant on Father's staff. When a fellow gets a commission and a new uniform he expects to be handled this way."

"In—in fun?" Ezra stared at him.

"Sure. Let him go, boys. He is a friend of mine."

Free, Ezra stood there and his face burned with shame as he looked from one to another of the smiling young soldiers.

"I've made a big fool of myself," he said honestly. "I'm asking you to excuse me for it."

"Gladly." The big fellow held out a muddy hand. "I am happy to make the acquaintance of a good fighter."

Then the others shook hands with him and went on their way.

"Kick me, Preston," Ezra said miserably.

Preston threw back his head and laughed. "I must change first. See you later."

"I'll be going along."

"Home?"

"No, not home. Never again."

"Oh." Preston raised his eyebrows. "I expected it, Ez."

"So'd I, but they didn't. I drove 'em out with a shotgun. They'll have me jugged if they can find me."

"Where are you going?"

"I don't know. I want to enlist, but they won't have me.'

"Who won't?"

"A soldier told me nobody gets into this army who ain't a gentleman."

"Then how did he get in?"

"I didn't think to ask him that." Ezra laughed.

"Have you seen Father about it?"

"No."

"His headquarters is in that tent." Preston jerked a thumb across the field. "The one with the palmetto flag."

"I can't walk in on a colonel."

"Of course you can. But not I, in this condition. Go ahead." Preston hurried away, oozing mud at every step.

Ezra walked over and stopped in front of the tent. It was guarded by a young and quite important-feeling soldier.

"Halt!"

"I have." Ezra grinned.

"Advance and give the countersign. No, that's what you do in the night." The soldier blushed in confusion. "What do you want?"

"I want to see Colonel Hampton."

"State your business."

"That's why I want to see him, to state my business."

"What is your name?" And when told he said, "Wait here. I will speak to the colonel." After a moment he came back and motioned Ezra inside.

Hampton sat at a field table, writing. He wore a perfectly plain gray uniform and looked larger than ever in the small tent.

"Well, well, Ezra!" He leaned back and smiled. "How is the leg?"

"All healed up, thank you, sir."

"What brings you here?"

The boy gave him the story in as few words as possible.

"Why do you want to be a soldier, Ezra?" the colonel asked.

"Because you advertised for men, sir."

"Not because your country needs you?"

"I figure you wouldn't be fighting if it wasn't necessary, sir."

"I consider it necessary." Hampton bit his mustache. "Which branch of the service do you wish to enter?"

"I lean toward the cavalry, sir."

"Our troopers usually furnish their own mounts. Do you have a horse?"

"No, sir."

"I fear the cavalry isn't for you, Ezra." Hampton saw keen disappointment in the boy's face, and added, "Why do you prefer it?"

"Well, sir, Ivanhoe rode a horse—and so do you."

The colonel knew hero worship when he saw it and, perhaps remembering his own youth, understood the fierce joy of it. He thought for a time.

"Orderly!" he called sharply.

"Yes, sir!" The soldier appeared at the door.

"Get me Private Festival Jones. You will find him with the horses."

"Yes, sir."

"Sit down, Ezra," Hampton said, returning to his writing. Officers and lesser people came and went for more than an hour before a bowlegged man appeared. He had a long, shaven face, bright blue eyes and generous ears covered with golden fuzz.

"Here I be, Colonel," he announced in a high-pitched voice, showing two solitary lower front teeth.

"Fess, this is Ezra Todd," Hampton said. "He knows nothing about horses and wishes to be a trooper. I want you to provide him with a mount and outfit and teach him how to use them. Give all your time to him for five days; then report to me."

"Yes, sir, Colonel." Fess was measuring Ezra up and down.

"Ezra," Hampton continued, "if you show promise you will be assigned to a troop, otherwise you go to the infantry. It is up to you."

"Thank you, sir." Ezra wondered if they could see his heart thumping. "I will work hard."

"You're darn right you will." Fess swung toward the door. "Come on, bub, you're in the army now."

Chapter 6

A S A matter of fact, during the next five days Ezra was not in sight of the army. Half an hour after leaving Colonel Hampton's tent he and Festival Jones were riding out of camp, carrying a skillet, coffee pot, tin cups and plates, provisions and blankets.

"Set up straight," Fess ordered under his breath. "You look like a case of persimmon bellyache."

"Yes, sir." Ezra stiffened his spine.

"Hold yore reins in yore *left* hand. T'other by yore side, stiff, not floppy like a dishrag."

"Yes, sir."

"Guess I'll take Spot." Fess looked around and whistled. "Where is that cussed dog? Oh, thar he is. Come on, Spot, come on!"

"I don't see any dog," Ezra said.

"Hain't none."

Without another word Fess led the way to the highway and on through the city. As they entered the country on the opposite side of town he broke into a trot with Ezra beside him. After a few rods he pulled his horse to a walk.

"And the colonel sez to me, 'Make a trooper of him in five days,' he sez!" Fess muttered. "Judas priest! Why'd he pick on me?"

"What are you talking about?" Ezra asked.

"You. You ride like a gander walkin' a rail fence in a high wind."

"I bet you wasn't so smooth the first time you rode a horse."

"Bub"—Fess looked at him sharply—"why'd you want to jine the cavalry?"

"I want to go along with Colonel Hampton," Ezra answered honestly.

"You like him?"

"I think he's a wonder."

"Judas priest, he is!" Fess slapped his horse. "And he can't have too many men round him that feel the same way. I'll larn you to ride or I'll hang yore hide on a hickory limb."

They turned into a lane and went up a low hill.

"Know whar you be?" Fess asked.

"Sure, this is part of *Sand Hills* plantation. But I don't know why we're here. I thought we were in the army."

"Bub," Fess said in a more friendly tone, "for some reason that hain't my business the colonel wants you in his troop, but you hain't up to snuff."

"I know, I'm not a gentleman," Ezra said hotly. "I've been told so before."

"Nonsense!" Fess snorted. "I hain't what they call a gentleman myself, but I can ride. That's what the colonel wants. Gentlemen can ride, too. That's why he's took so many of 'em —'cause they can ride, not 'cause they're gentlemen. What's more, they fetch their own hosses."

"I haven't a horse."

"The colonel will take care of that. He's spent a heap of his own money on his regiment. Iffen you show him you can ride, he'll see you have the outfit."

"Then why don't I drill with the others and learn to ride?"

"Bub, iffen you was to try ridin' with them fellers now you'd be a laughin' stock. The colonel don't want that. He'd cut off his right hand 'fore he'd humilify a friend."

"How do you know all this?" Ezra asked bluntly. "Who are you?"

"I'm Festival Jones from Cashier's Valley, North Caroliny. I thought you knowed it."

"I didn't, and it don't mean anything to me now."

"You see, bub," Fess explained in a patient voice, "the Hamptons own a big farm up thar 'n' they raise cattle 'n' sheep 'n' such like. The colonel 'n' his father spent a lot of time thar workin' 'n' huntin' 'n' fishin'. Sence we was boys the colonel 'n' me sort of run wild thar, like two hound pups."

"I begin to see," Ezra interjected.

"Yeh. They started a school 'n' I larned to read 'n' write. They tried to larn me to talk proper, but that didn't take. So you see, when I heard Wade—that's the colonel—was raisin' a regiment I hotfooted it down."

Ezra said nothing for a few moments, but just sat thinking about the chance Colonel Hampton had given him, the no-account boy from down the creek.

"How are you going to teach me to ride in five days?" he finally asked.

"We're goin' to camp in the back pasture 'n' work."

"Did the colonel tell you to come here?"

"You heard what he said. I'm to larn you to set a hoss. How I do it's my business."

"What are we waiting for?"

"For you to run out of talk." Fess rose in his stirrups and looked around. "Whar's that dog?"

"You said there is no dog."

"Thar hain't."

"What ails you, anyway?"

"Bub," Fess said solemnly, "Festival Jones is odder'n Job's off ox. Allus remember that 'n' you'll understand him better."

"But what about the dog?"

"His name is Spot. I left him in Cashier's Valley 'cause a war hain't no place for a dog to be in. But I'm mighty fond of Spot 'n' thar hain't no reason I can't pertend he's with me for company. Understand?"

"Not exactly. But it don't matter."

"Not a mite," Fess agreed and led the way down the hill.

During those ensuing five days Ezra learned more about horses than some people do in as many years. His world was a pasture beyond sight of highways and dwellings, peopled solely by himself and Fess and ruthlessly dominated by the latter. Fess was a master horseman and a relentless teacher whose only thought was to do the work Colonel Hampton had given him to do. He had said he would teach the boy to ride or kill him, and before long Ezra wondered which it would be.

The boy had worked hard for Jed Sears, but never like this. He crawled out of his blanket before dawn to feed and groom the horses and he crawled back, sore and lame, after dark.

"Rich boys'll have servants to do such work, but you won't," Fess explained. "So larn it now."

"But why is it necessary to curry a horse way out here beyond sight of everybody?" Ezra wanted to know.

"This is why, bub." Fess paused in building the breakfast fire. "A hoss has got pride 'n' self-respect same as folkses has. Iffen he knows he looks good it makes him feel good 'n' he thanks his master. A hoss that's ashamed of hisself won't do his best for the man who rides him."

"All right," Ezra conceded. "But I don't see the sense in polishing the saddles and bridles when we're the only ones to look at them."

"Judas priest! Hain't we enough?" Fess glared at him. "Man who hain't got pussonal pride, who thinks only of showin' off to other folkses, hain't fitten to ride a jackass. Don't let me hear no more such talk outen you. Understand?"

"Yes. But I still think—"

"Nary mind what *you* think. Colonel Hampton thinks you've got the makin's of a trooper, else you wouldn't be here now. Want to shame him, do you, when we go back to camp?"

"Of course I don't."

"Then keep yore mind on yore work."

Ezra did just that, and what monotonous work it was! He learned how to mount and dismount, to grip his horse with his knees, how to hold his hands, his feet, his shoulders, his head, all of it to be repeated over and over and over, until his whole body became a machine whose several parts clicked into place when it was set in motion. Hours, days of this while walking his horse, then the almost hopeless attempt to do those things at a trot, a canter, a gallop. Back and forth across the pasture, up and down the hills, stopping, starting, turning, jumping low hurdles, then higher ones, always under the pitiless eyes of Fess, whose criticism, except on rare occasions, was not laudatory. More and more and more of it, until his muscles throbbed with pain and his mind reeled when he finally fell asleep under the stars.

The fifth morning came, and somewhat to his surprise Ezra was not only alive but glad of it.

"For all you tried so hard, you couldn't kill me." He grinned across the coffeepot at Fess.

"You're an ungrateful cuss," Fess commented, tossing a ham bone to the phantom Spot.

"No, I'm not. I've learned a lot, even if I wind up in the infantry."

"Infantry—walkin' soldiers! They won't git to the war 'fore it's all over."

"You think it won't last long?"

"One battle."

"The Yanks aren't that easy!"

"How do you know?"

"Well, my people were from the North."

"No!" Fess gave him a hard look. "How come you're here?"

Ezra gave him the story.

"Judas priest! Mebbe it'll take two battles," Fess said. Which was a compliment to Ezra.

That afternoon, with the last buckle polished and every

horsehair in place, they cantered into camp beyond Columbia. The place was even busier than before, but Ezra saw only Colonel Hampton, standing in front of his tent talking with another officer. The boy's heart pounded as he saw the colonel had recognized them and was watching their approach. This was the test, for Hampton could measure a man at a glance. They pulled up and saluted with a snap. Hampton returned the salute and came forward a few steps.

"Mission accomplished, Jones?" he asked gravely.

"Yes, Colonel."

"Result satisfactory?"

"Yes, Colonel."

"Excellent! Todd, report to the quartermaster for your uniform and equipment."

"Yes, sir!" To Ezra neither the war nor anything else mattered then.

Before night he had his uniform and, as he looked down at the soft gray with its gilded buttons and braid, he felt he had attained the peak of earthly glory. Ivanhoe in shining armor was never so proud. Weapons were hard to get that early in the war, but Hampton had already armed his men, largely at his own expense. The infantry had rifles and bayonets, the cavalry, pistols and straight two-edged swords made in Columbia. The colonel carried the same kind of blade, only larger to match his gigantic strength—it was forty inches long and weighed six pounds. To his adoring troops it was made of legendary stuff, a sort of modern *Excalibur* that would hew a path straight to Washington in short order.

There followed days of hard drilling, glorious days for

Ezra. He found himself accepted by the young troopers, if not quite as an equal, at least as a partner in this business of war. The whole thing was a lark for them, and they threw themselves into it as though it must be enjoyed to the full because it would soon be over. They worked and played with gusto and the way they spent money staggered Ezra. Every day each of them threw away more than he would receive as a month's pay—eleven dollars.

That was their affair. His was to make good in Hampton's Legion. As a horseman he was by no means the equal of his fellow troopers, most of whom had been raised in the saddle, but, by constant observation and application of what he learned, he managed not to disgrace his outfit. Nights, and in spare moments, Fess briefed him on his duties, and Fess had a surprising knowledge of how to get along in the army. The Hamptons, both the colonel and Lieutenant Preston, made no further obvious efforts in Ezra's behalf. He had made the grade and been accepted as a trooper. His progress was now up to him without benefit of favoritism. That was what he wanted; in fact, one of his main worries at first was being known as the colonel's pet. That was over now. He was standing on his own feet and competing on equal terms with the rest of them.

Meanwhile, the war was actually flaring along the Potomac. Virginia had seceded. Robert E. Lee had refused to serve in the Union Army, and troops were gathering at Richmond, the new capital of the Confederacy. Hampton's Legion was ready to move when it got orders.

There came a day—it was the twenty-fourth of June—when

Ezra did his turn as guard in front of the colonel's tent. It was a routine job, merely to keep sight-seers from getting under foot, but he felt rather important with the authority to order civilians around. Girls sighed at sight of his smart uniform, old gentlemen asked respectful questions, ladies smiled at the brave young soldier—all very pleasing to the lad from down the creek.

His thoughts returned to the shack in the clearing and so, for an instant, it seemed natural to see Jed and Bert approaching. When he realized who they were he stiffened and waited.

"Halt!" he snapped when they moved toward the tent.

"Jeez!" Bert's mouth fell open in the old familiar way. "Hit's Ez, Pa!"

Jed stared, then rolled his cud of tobacco and grinned.

"All purtied up, too! Ez, this's the sheriff." He stuck out a thumb toward a stout man. "Tell him what we're hyar fer, sheriff."

The stout man, who recognized the headquarters tent, hesitated before he asked, "Be you Ezra Todd?"

"I am," Ezra answered curtly.

"Well, as—as an officer of the law, I've got business with you."

"As you see, I am on duty." Ezra glared at him.

"Yeh, yeh, that's so. Well, when'll you be free?"

"When the war is over."

"Well, now—well—"

"Talk up to him," Jed growled. "He cain't hide behind them purty clo'es."

"He hain't no better'n he ever wuz," Bert added.

"Well"—the sheriff shifted his feet—"as an officer of the law I've got a warrant for yer arrest on the charge of attempted murder with a shotgun on the persons of these two gent'men."

"Take him right hyar 'n' now," Jed demanded loudly.

"Or we'll complain uv you," Bert threatened.

"If I were you," Ezra said to the sheriff in a confidential tone, "I wouldn't be too fast about picking up Colonel Hampton's sentry."

"Well—well—" The officer was plainly in a pickle. "There ain't nothin' pussonal in this."

"Hit's pussonal with me!" Jed shouted. "He drawed a shotgun on me and I'll have the law on him."

"Me, too!" Bert declared.

Four troopers were passing and Ezra smiled to himself when he saw that Fess was among them.

"Private Jones," he ordered sharply, "these people are a nuisance. You will escort them off the field."

"Yes, sir!" Fess swung about smartly.

"We won't go!" Jed doubled his fists.

"You won't?" Fess scowled ferociously and drew his sword. "Shove 'em along, boys." He nodded to his companions.

As they were being marched away, Preston stepped out of the tent and poked Ezra in the ribs.

"Is that the way to use friends you may never see again?" His eyes twinkled.

"I expect to see them again," Ezra answered.

"You never can tell." Preston jigged with excitement. "We have our marching orders. We leave for Richmond this afternoon."

Chapter 7

EZRA gathered from Preston's enthusiastic words that the legion would board the train with the ease of a picnic party. Neither of them appreciated the job of entraining a thousand soldiers and nearly as many body servants, hundreds of cavalry and artillery horses, and endless equipment. A majority of the young bloods had brought a great deal of luggage, as though going to war were a holiday. As a matter of fact it took days, and the colonel, who was among the last to leave, did not get away until the fourth of July.

When each contingent was ready to go the proud ladies of Columbia presented its members with personal gifts. They were, for the most part, as valueless as they were well intended. Though Ezra and Fess had neither relatives nor personal friends in the city, they were not forgotten. When they went aboard the cars each carried a package wrapped in gay paper and tied with ribbon enough to hang a cat. Fess even had a bunch of flowers.

"Don't I look sweet?" He stuck the bouquet under his nose and simpered foolishly. Then, as they happened to be alone in a boxcar, he tossed the flowers out the farther door.

"What's your other beauty prize?" Ezra wanted to know.

"Feels like a grindstone." Fess pulled off the wrapping. "Judas priest! A pound cake! Weighs ten pounds, now that's a present! Eat it or bust a Yank with it. What you got, bub?"

"How do I know?" Ezra unwrapped an oblong linen case embroidered with forget-me-nots. "What the heck is it?"

" 'Tain't eatable, by the looks. Open it up."

Ezra took off the cover and fished out a card inscribed in curlicue writing:

> *May all your fears be mild as doves,*
> *And may this case protect your gloves.*

"A glove case!" Fess leaned against the car weakly. "You're a gentleman now, mister. Ain't that nice!"

"My gosh, it's scented!" Ezra hurled it out the door.

"What a pity!" Fess made a sad, clucking noise. "I could've used it to carry my plug terbacker. Wouldn't it have been somethin' to chaw heliotrope terbacker! Chance of a lifetime gone."

By then more troopers were entering the car, so he broke the cake into chunks and passed them around.

"Youah hands ah dirty, suh," objected a finicky young dandy.

"So ah youah mannahs, suh," Fess mimicked, and as the train started laughter drowned out the youngster's reply.

It was Ezra's first train ride. He found it a stirring experience, being in a house that tore along faster than a horse could trot. The boys smashed holes in the sides of the cars with their carbine butts and, sticking their heads out, whooped and sang the miles away. War was a lark and weren't they lucky to be in on it! At every station where they stopped pretty girls handed out food and drinks, so the celebration picked up tempo with mileage. It was against orders to ride on top of the cars, but orders were made for civilians, not for heroes on their way to battle. They were privileged personages, these elite men of Hampton's Legion, and they rode where they pleased. And they did pretty much as they pleased. They pelted each other, and occasionally spectators, with fruit and vegetables. They emptied their canteens from car roofs onto protruding heads below. They fired at crows and buzzards and sometimes took a pot shot at a sleepy mule or cow. The only trouble with this war was that it wouldn't last long, so they must make the most of it.

When they finally reached Richmond, wearied by the ride and the monkeyshines, they were met by a band and marched out to their camp east of the city. Immediately Hampton set them to drilling mercilessly and enforced discipline so strictly that it annoyed many of the young aristocrats. They had enlisted to fight, not maneuver endlessly in the hot sun all day and stand sentry at night. But they took it—they had to or lose face, something no Southern gentleman could do. The colonel ignored their grumbling, for he knew this was no stage war. A Northern army was already crossing the Potomac less than a hundred miles away and General Beauregard of the Confederate Army was waiting for it at Manassas Junction. There was no time to waste.

On July nineteen Hampton got orders to join Beauregard. The news crackled through camp and the young soldiers in gray whooped; this would be the end of the war and they were in on time. At the same moment thirty thousand other young soldiers, in blue, were laughing and singing their way from Washington toward Richmond. They, too, were sure the war would be over in a few days, as soon as they had knocked the Johnny Rebs into a cocked hat and taken their capital.

The tents of Hampton's Legion were being struck when the headquarters telegraph clicked out orders that were at first unbelievable: only the six hundred infantry would go to the front. There was no transportation available for cavalry and artillery. The troopers, who were already known far and wide as the snappiest, best-drilled and best-equipped unit of the Confederate Army, were to sit at home while the great blow was being delivered.

Colonel Hampton galloped to the War Office in Richmond, where the news was verified; there were barely enough cars to carry the infantry, none at all for horses. He appealed to Jefferson Davis, but the Confederate president was not a magician to produce boxcars out of the air. Hampton offered to lead his troops to the front in forced marches and was told that, even if he arrived in time, his four hundred horsemen would make little difference to Beauregard who had twenty-two thousand men. Very politely he was given to understand it was his place to obey, not question, orders. Deeply hurt, but taking it like a soldier, he went back to camp and put the infantry aboard the train.

For thirty hours they rode the slow, bumping cars that seemed to go in every direction except ahead. When they finally stopped at Manassas Junction the first men Hampton saw were troopers Festival Jones and Ezra Todd, sitting on the roof of a car.

"Come down here," he ordered sharply.

They dropped to the ground and saluted briskly.

"What are you doing here?"

"We're on leave, Colonel," Fess answered easily.

And Ezra added, in a less confident tone, "We have the written permission of our captain, sir."

"Explain." Hampton looked tired and travel-stained and in no mood for levity. "I will be with you in a moment," he said aside to Lieutenant Colonel Johnson. "Preston is contacting Beauregard for orders. Now, Fess?"

"Well, Colonel, when we see things wouldn't be rushin' fer a spell with us, we applied to the captain fer three days' leave to visit friends. He said yes, so here we be."

"You are visiting friends *here*?"

"Shore, Colonel, all these boys're our friends."

"In other words, you hope to take part in the battle."

"We-ll," Fess rubbed his chin, "bein' guests in town, we aim to do as our friends do."

"Fess, you rascal!" Hampton's eyes twinkled. "Actually you are disobeying orders, but technically you are within your rights."

"That's just exactly what we figured," Fess answered, and Ezra was aghast to see him wink at the colonel.

It was dusk when the legionnaires got settled in camp. The "guests" were given food and blankets, though there were some pointed questions as to how two cavalrymen, armed but without horses, happened to be with the outfit. It was a long time before Ezra went to sleep. There was not much noise, but he sensed the presence of many men—an army—and as the circle of his imagination widened, two armies, for not far away were thirty thousand Yankees. But he was young and tired, and eventually he slept.

It was Sunday morning when he was awakened by a distant rumbling. At first he thought it was thunder, then he noticed that the sky was bright.

"Is that cannon?" he asked a soldier who was rolling up a blanket near by.

"Sure. The Yanks are attacking along Bull Run."

"Attacking us?"

"Attacking Bee and Evans, who are dug in on the south bank."

It meant little to Ezra, though he assumed Bull Run was a stream that separated the armies. He picked up his gun and looked around, experiencing that helpless feeling a soldier knows while waiting for orders. Everyone was in motion, doing a thousand little things to keep busy. Cooking fires were crackling and soon bread and bacon held the soldiers' attention, while the throbbing thunder rolled up out of the north. As the men ate, some of them talked and joked nervously and others stared silently at the lightening sky. Some could not eat at all and walked up and down, making sharp turns as though drilling. A few were writing letters. The sun edged up over the eastern hills and the valley mist trembled, then silently dissolved. It was going to be a hot day.

Ezra was squatting on his heels when a long roll on the drum brought him up standing. There was the crash of hundreds of tin cups and plates as the men snatched their arms and began falling in by companies. Colonel Hampton on a big horse and Lieutenant Colonel Johnson on a smaller one were talking with other officers in the road. Soldiers near them caught some of the conversation and word ran through the ranks that they were to defend or attack Stone Bridge. No one was sure which, or where the bridge was, but it didn't matter—the time for action had come.

Hampton sent Preston galloping away with a message, then pivoted his horse and looked over the camp, waiting. Subordinate officers snapped orders right and left, getting their men in line.

"Shake a leg, bub," Ezra heard Fess say behind him. "We come to fight, not gawp."

"We haven't been assigned to a company."

"You got to have a letter from Jeff Davis 'fore you can h'ist a foot? Git in here 'side uv me 'n' shut up."

A company was passing in double column and they fell in at its rear.

"Keep step, you galoot!" Fess growled. "We're in the infantry now. Walk's I do."

"I can't walk as you do, I'm not bowlegged," Ezra retorted.

"Silence in the ranks!" a sergeant barked. In the midst of hundreds of talking men that was funny and the company laughed.

"Halt!" someone shouted up ahead.

Ezra nearly ran down the man in front, who grinned over his shoulder forgivingly. Craning their necks to learn what was going on, they saw Colonel Hampton wave his great two-edged sword and start walking his horse down the road. The legion band broke into *Dixie*, orders cracked about the field, and the regiment was off to battle.

It was two and a half miles to the stream called Bull Run, through a pleasant land of farms and woodlands. The sun was hot, but the South Carolinians liked it; everything was perfect, including the menacing thunder of the guns, and in accordance with their dreams of war.

"Scairt, bub?" Fess whispered, when they were close enough to distinguish the rattle of small arms.

"Sick to my stomach," Ezra confessed. "You?"

"Sweatin' like a bull hookin' a root."

"I'm not so afraid of getting hit as I am that I'll run away."

"Southerners don't run away," Fess answered confidently.

No? Then what were those gray troops doing on the ridge beyond the Warrenton Turnpike? If they weren't cutting for the rear as fast as they could go, the points of the compass were sadly confused. And behind them were lines of cheering bluecoats. This wasn't the sort of thing the plans called for.

Hampton, who had been scouting ahead, galloped back and ordered his men to take cover behind the roadside fences and open fire. So they did as the battered, bloody remnant of Bee's and Evans' troops pounded past them, too demoralized to see that they now had a chance to retrieve their honor. The Federals came close behind, but the men from South Carolina were shooting straight and the blue lines slowed, stopped, and stood to return the fire. They, too, could shoot and within five minutes Lieutenant Colonel Johnson lay dead in the road. Then cannon opened up from both Northern flanks.

Ezra lay behind a rail fence, loading, firing, and yelling. Of a sudden he was in the very center of a combined hailstorm and thunderstorm of lead and iron. Bullets buzzed and whined overhead, plunked into the rails on each side, kicked dirt into his eyes. A cannon ball knocked over two posts, letting the fence collapse. Shrapnel burst so close that his temples throbbed with pain. It seemed impossible that anything the size of a man could live there, yet he was alive, exultantly, defiantly alive. He didn't know he was yelling, didn't know he was forgetting to bite the ends off the paper cartridges before ramming them home, so they did not explode when he pulled the trigger. When the barrel was full and he realized what he had done he jumped up and threw the gun as far as he could at the enemy.

"Git down, you fool!" Fess yelled.

He dropped behind the fence and looked around. On his left the soldier who had smiled back at him as they fell in line lay dead. Ezra began to tremble, then to sob. Death was walking on the field but this was the first time it had stopped beside him. It had touched this man and taken from him everything he had ever known and felt and hoped for. Ezra lay on his face and cried, not because he had lost a companion but because he was afraid. He wanted to get away, so far away he would never hear another gun as long as he lived.

He raised his head and looked cautiously down the line, trying to figure out a safe route of retreat. If he could crawl to the woods he would head south until he was beyond the reach of war. Let men kill each other if they must, slavery, states rights and secession meant nothing to him. But Wade Hampton did mean something to him. There, squarely in the middle of the road, the colonel was riding calmly toward him. The very sight of such courage was enough to put heart into any man. As Ezra watched he caught his breath, for the big bay horse was staggering toward the side of the road. As he went down Hampton jumped clear. He started toward the ditch, then turned, pulled his pistol and shot the suffering animal behind the ear. He loved horses and this one had been his favorite hunter. Then he walked to the fence, picked up a fallen rifle and began firing. Ezra shook his head and crawled over to the dead man on his left, muttering to himself. He took the rifle from the lifeless hands, transferred the cartridges to his own box, and faced the enemy.

History says that this stubborn stand of Hampton's six hundred men gave the first check to McDowell's flank attack and quite possibly won the battle of Bull Run. But to the troops themselves, under fire for the first time and desperately busy, it did not look like a victory. Outnumbered and without artillery support, the line was under fearful pressure along its whole length. Still it held and might have done so to the last man if it had not been ordered to fall back. The legionnaires had seen enough of shameful running away so they retreated slowly and in order, holding the Federals off with a steady fire. Only two men broke under the strain, dropped their rifles, and disappeared forever, as Ezra had wanted to do. He saw them both in full flight but had no desire to join them. Because he knew how they felt, he made no attempt to shoot them down as some of the others did.

Hampton, still on foot and still using his borrowed rifle, collected his command in a little valley, then moved up a hill to some pine trees to line up with a Virginia regiment. Ezra looked around a tree trunk and saw a tall, erect, bearded officer surveying the field as calmly as though it were a cabbage patch. It was the boy's first sight of General Jackson who, at that very moment, was earning his immortal sobriquet of "Stonewall," though no one knew it at the time.

"Judas priest, it's hot!" said a voice behind the next tree, and Ezra edged over beside Fess.

"You all right, Fess?"

"Alive, if that's what you mean."

"Wounded?"

"No. You?"

"No. I don't see how any of us escaped."

"Must be after noon. Lordy, I'm hungry. Seen Spot?"

"Spot? Oh, your dog. No." Ezra smiled.

"I'm afraid the Yanks got him. It worries me."

"I wish I had nothing to worry about except an imaginary dog." Ezra bit the end off a cartridge and rammed it home. "How do you think the fight is going?"

"Seems like we've stopped the varmints. But I can't see no more what's goin' on than you can."

"I don't see how the officers know."

"There's a stiddy stream of messengers goin' back 'n' forth like bees to a molasses jug."

Lying there in the pines, taking and returning the fire of the blue lines on the other ridge, Hampton's Legion knew little about the battle except what it could see, but it looked as though they held a key position, for regiments and parts of regiments were coming up to reinforce them. From the new arrivals they learned of desperate fighting elsewhere. As neither side yet had the upper hand it must be the despised Yankees could really stand up to it. General Beauregard was in command here and rode up and down, talking with officers, and gesticulating profusely after the manner of Frenchmen. Since forcing the surrender of Fort Sumter he had been a hero and he was now working hard to hold his reputation.

The afternoon heat was terrific. Ezra had never realized before that shooting a rifle could be hard work, but as the day wore on he sweated and ached as he had never done in Jed's cornfield. It occurred to him, with some surprise, that he was no longer afraid and had buckled down to fighting as to any other job that must be done. Something must be wrong; this wasn't war as he had pictured it. Where was the thrill and glory and sense of sacrifice and all the other heroics? There was noise and shouting, wounded men and dead, yet somehow the wild exultation of battle was not there. He was too calm. This shooting at distant men was almost like target practice, wholly lacking in the element of personal combat.

Then came a change. Suddenly cannon balls began tearing through the forest, plowing the turf and spattering men around like ripe fruit. A human head rolled out of the bushes beside Ezra and he never saw the body to which it belonged.

"They've moved up their batteries!" a captain shouted.

Beauregard and Jackson galloped past. A few minutes later there was a wild yell on the left and a regiment of Virginia cavalry swept through the woods and down the hill. Ezra got a fleeting look at the cocky young colonel who led them, and heard a Virginia rifleman yell, "That's Jeb Stuart! He'll knock hell out of 'em!"

Beauregard was back, standing in his stirrups and pointing with his sword at the Federal position. Hampton roared an order at his officers and was off after the cavalry. From end to end the whole Confederate line swayed forward, the excitement of battle sweeping it like fire in dry grass. Ezra forgot to shoot, forgot everything except that he was one of thousands, part of a great irresistible force of destruction. This was it! This was the madness that Ivanhoe and the Black Knight and all other warriors had known through the ages.

They went down into the valley and up the other side. The cavalry had chopped the Union line badly, but it was still fighting back, its cannon blazing point-blank into the charging mass. Hampton fell. Captain Conner, the only senior officer left in the regiment, leaped into the lead and led the charge on the guns. The regimental color-bearer went down and Beauregard himself caught up the flag.

Such men could not be stopped. The Federal line broke— more than broke—it became a terrified mob. The panic spread across the field, and before sundown McDowell's proud army was on the run toward Washington. Even William Tecumseh Sherman, who was an unknown then, had to ride hard to escape capture.

The Confederates pursued until weariness halted them. They lay on the grass and in the wheat fields and orchards, panting like winded dogs, then slowly began garnering the harvest about them. Guns, ammunition, uniforms, haversacks, personal belongings of every kind had been abandoned by the thousands.

Ezra ate supper with some boys from Georgia who were having a high time with a load of captured provisions and a keg of Yankee whisky. He took a small drink and lay down, believing himself to be the most weary person who ever trod the earth. But he could not sleep because the battle was still going on in his mind, an endless procession of men and horses and waving flags, sounds of command, cries of the wounded and roaring of the guns. Did people ever sleep again after passing through battle? Did a man ever pull himself together after he had seen his idolized commander go down? Damn the Yankees! He hoped ten thousand of them were dead, though a million would not be worth one Wade Hampton.

Gradually, from sheer exhaustion, those about him fell silent. Ezra thought of working his way back to camp but could not bear to pass among the dead and dying in the dark. When daylight came—

"Spot, here, Spot!" a voice called near by.

"Fess!" he shouted. "Are you there?" Ezra stood up and stared off into the dark.

"Pretty likely. But where's that cussed dog? I've got a bone for him."

"You idiot! Come over here."

"Hurt, bub?" Fess was approaching.

"No."

"Lonesome?"

"I don't feel very chipper with the colonel dead."

"Dead, your granny! He only got a wallop on the head. He's good as new."

Weak with relief, Ezra sat down, and of a sudden the day's work caught up with him and he slept.

Chapter 8

THE battle of Manassas, or Bull Run, was a Confederate victory but it dispelled all Southern hope of a short war. The Federals had behaved disgracefully at the end, yet every Johnny Reb knew that plenty of his comrades had done no better earlier, and the fight had been touch and go all the way through. In the field each side had learned respect for the other, and at home both nations realized that a long struggle lay ahead. Abraham Lincoln appointed George B. McClellan commander of the Army of the Potomac and Jefferson Davis became aware that Joseph E. Johnston, Stonewall Jackson, J. E. B. Stuart, and Wade Hampton were real leaders.

Johnston, for all he was a hard man to work with, was placed at the head of the army defending Richmond, and Hampton's Legion, as part of his right wing, camped at Bacon Race Church, nine miles from Manassas Junction. The Yankees were again south of the Potomac, and the two armies, whose pickets were within shouting distance of each other, settled down to a period of skirmishing and drilling, as boxers go into training for the next bout. There was action on other fronts, but this held the major interest, for a breakthrough in either direction might well be decisive.

Hampton's gay young gentlemen were as brave as men ever were and would cheerfully have followed their colonel if the regiment had been ordered to charge the whole Union Army alone. In fact, those youngsters, who had been raised on the Walter Scott brand of chivalry, half expected something of the kind to happen. Consequently, when they were told to dig rifle pits and latrines, when they were practically reduced to the status of field hands, they got the shock of their lives. Few of them had ever touched a pick or shovel, but to their honor they learned how to use such tools that summer. Sweat and dirt took the sheen off the handsome uniforms and, as the boys became tough and realistic, war lost the glamour their idealism had lent it and became just plain hard work. They threw away their superfluous luggage, sent home their useless body servants, and found pride in the fact that they could stand on their own feet and take care of themselves. The pampered lads came through like men.

To Ezra and the few others who were accustomed to work, the transition was not painful. In a way it was pleasant, for it removed the artificial barriers of caste and put all the men on the same level. The boy who could read Latin and wore silk underwear might retain the polish of a gentleman, but to him a man like Festival Jones was no longer a boor but an envied comrade who could shovel with either hand without changing the position of his feet. For the first time in their lives some of the gentry understood what down-to-earth friendship meant.

There were some who would never understand. They were the "gentlemen of the old South, suh" type, not numerous but so odious they gave a bad smell to the whole state from which they came. Hampton had no sympathy for such.

There was a Georgian named Temple who believed his family's wealth placed him beyond the reach of camp law. The colonel had warned that pillaging or other forms of molestation committed by his men against civilians would be punished. The rule was hardly necessary, for most of the troopers respected personal property and the complaints noted were so petty as to be charged to local rascals. Hampton did not believe that his men would steal trousers off a line or eggs from a hen's nest, but when an old lady burst into camp one morning before breakfast, to say she had seen a soldier making off with her red rooster, he decided to investigate. The troops were paraded, the camp police searched the tents and found the unplucked carcass of the rooster under Temple's blanket.

Hampton called the Georgian out of line and looked him up and down. "You stole this fowl?" he asked.

"Yes, sir."

"Were you prompted by hunger to do so?"

"No, sir."

"Are you a habitual chicken thief?"

"Sir"—Temple's face was redder than the rooster—"I con-sider that a—"

"Answer my question!" Hampton thundered.

"Yes, sir. No, sir. I did it as a prank." The soldier tried to smile ingratiatingly, but Hampton interrupted.

"Flouting the orders of your officers is not a prank," he said sternly. "Nor is it a prank to deprive a poor woman of a por-tion of her property."

"I will reimburse her, sir."

"Do so at once."

Temple settled with the woman in cold hauteur.

"Now I suppose the ridiculous incident is closed," he remarked impertinently to the colonel.

For an instant Hampton's eyes blazed. "Corporal," he ordered one of the provost guards, "hang the fowl about Private Temple's neck and see that he wears it for the remainder of the day."

"Yes, sir!" The corporal grinned.

Throughout the rest of that day the gentleman from Georgia went about his work with the rooster dangling against his chest and on all sides he heard the flapping of wings and shrill repetitions of the most hated sounds on earth —"Cock-a-doodle-do!"

Such incidents broke the routine of camp life, which was becoming monotonous for even the most enthusiastic legionnaires. Hampton chafed because his cavalry was not given more work to do. He felt that all the mounted troops were wasting their talents in unrelated efforts; they should be assembled in one unit and trained to strike smashing blows. But the high command was not ready to listen to him. In fact, during that first summer he and Jefferson Davis were not on the best of terms and the colonel was considerably neglected. He did not sulk, but he deplored his inactivity and wrote his wife: *There is never anything to tell you.*

Not that the legion was allowed to rust. Hampton knew the day was not far off when every man in the South would be needed in battle and he gave all his energy to preparing his command for that time. He bought arms in England with his own money, supplied uniforms, and even stripped his estates of horses for his cavalry. Furthermore, though it was not generally known, he offered the government a million and a half dollars' worth of cotton from his Mississippi plantations, an offer that was held up by red tape and political jealousy until it was worthless.

Meanwhile, the colonel kept his men drilling until they became highly efficient on the parade ground. This gave Ezra his chance and he made the most of it. Starting with what Fess had taught him, he went on until he became more than an average trooper, which was high praise in that company. Regardless of what lay ahead, he knew he had already fought and won his greatest battle.

So the summer wore on. Great events were shaping farther south and west but the Army of Northern Virginia was mainly concerned with its own affairs. There was no real fighting, yet men died by thousands from disease. Had a major battle occurred, half the troops would have been unfit for duty. Hardly a soldier was free from dysentery and one in seven had measles, an illness seldom fatal in itself but likely to lead to deadly complications. Malaria was everywhere and typhoid and pneumonia were justly dreaded far more than Yankee bullets.

The causes of this deplorable condition were myriad. In the first place, men were allowed to enlist without physical examinations. Any male from fifteen to seventy-five who could stand on two feet and carry a gun was permitted to take the field. Naturally great numbers of them could not stand the gaff. The weather was hot and the troops drank wherever they found water, even from roadside puddles. And, too, for all the boasting about Southern cooking, camp fare was poor. Flapjacks with salted or smoked meat, and these not too well prepared, were the main dishes month after month. Vegetables were rarely seen and fruit, when there was any, was usually too green or too ripe. It took a tough digestive system to stand up under such treatment.

Since there was no known connection between vermin and disease the camp was alive with mosquitoes, flies, fleas and lice, which accounted for many of the health problems.

"Iffen we could only tease the cusses to enlist," Fess said wearily one night when they were trying to sleep. "These muskeeters 're plenty big 'nough to shoulder a musket. What flyin' soldiers they'd be!" He slapped and swore vigorously.

"You got one," Ezra said from under the blanket he had pulled over his head. "I felt the ground tremble when he dropped."

"Yeh, but a hunderd'll come to his wake."

"Never mind, they'll clear out in the morning when the flies come."

"They have to, there hain't standin' room for them 'n' the flies too."

"They pester the Yanks same as us, that's one comfort."

"Nossir, Abe Lincoln's blue-bellies're so full of poor rum a muskeeter dassn't bite one."

"Shucks!"

Autumn, then winter came while the two armies faced each other, for the most part inactively. The public on both sides clamored for action. Still the cautious McClellan and the unready Johnston waited, built up their supplies and drilled their troops. In November, Hampton was made an acting brigadier and given command of three regiments in addition to his own. His commission did not come through for several months, but he was considered a general and addressed as such. His legionnaires were proud of his promotion but they no longer went in for heroic speeches. Hard work, sickness, and the knowledge that the Yankees were no pushover had sobered them. It had also strengthened them; they had replaced their pretty caps with sensible felt hats, owners of a thousand slaves took their turns at cooking, and pampered sons, once top-heavy with pride, curried a sick comrade's horse without asking its owner's social rating.

Ezra endured the winter without great distress, for he was naturally healthy and was accustomed to hardship. Furthermore, Fess was a good cook and Preston Hampton was forever slipping them choice eatables that had been sent up from *Sand Hills*. The boy was neither homesick nor worried about business as many were. Army life was far better than what he had known at the Searses and he was trying hard to forget what lay behind him.

On a warm afternoon in early March he did his go at picket duty along a brook that separated the two armies. Sentries on both sides fraternized more or less openly so he was not surprised to be hailed by a Federal from the other bank. "Nice day, Johnny Reb."

"Good enough," Ezra agreed.

"Sugar weather we call it back home."

"You don't make sugar in the north, Yank."

"Sure we do, maple sugar. Ever hear of it?"

"No."

"Gosh! Say, Johnny, you won't shoot me if I fetch you over a hunk?"

"No, come on over, blue-belly."

The Northerner jumped the brook and from his pocket pulled a cake of maple sugar wrapped in paper. "Try it." He broke off a piece and held it out. "It was made on our farm in Vermont. Mother sent it to me."

Ezra bit into it and nodded. "Good! How do you make it?"

"Sit down and I'll tell you."

They sat on a log, with their rifles between their knees, and the Federal soldier explained about tapping maple trees and boiling the sap until it was sugar. He was only a boy and half sick with longing for home.

"Gosh, it's good up there now!" he said wistfully. "The sun is shining through the treetops and the robins are hollering and the old sugarhouse is steaming like a teakettle." He winked the tears back. "Say, Johnny, why are we fighting a war?"

"Oh!" Ezra looked at the sky. "Slavery—states rights—you know."

"Yeh, I know what the politicians say, but why are *we* fighting—you and me? I don't want to shoot you and you don't want to shoot me. It's the same with thousands and thousands of other fellers. Why do we do it?"

"Cussed if I know, Yank."

"Just as I thought."

"You got plenty of tobacco?"

"Well, no. My money's gone and the sutler won't trust nobody."

"Here." Ezra handed him a sack.

"Gosh, thanks! You know what I'm going to do with it? I'm going to send it to my father and write him it's a personal gift from a Johnny Reb."

"He probably hates all Southerners."

"Oh, sure. He's never seen one."

"It's a queer world, Yank."

"Ain't it, though! You'd like my folks and they'd like you, yet—"

A bullet plunked into the log between them and a musket roared across the brook.

"I'll kill that fool!" the Northerner cried, as they jumped up.

"Get back on your side," Ezra whispered. "That'll bring an officer and you don't want to be caught here."

"Thanks, Johnny." The boy jumped the brook and disappeared in the underbrush.

A man appeared for an instant on the side of the hill and then was gone. Ezra took a snap shot at him and knew he missed. As he stepped behind a tree to reload he wondered how it was that the gait of the Yankee soldier had seemed familiar.

Chapter 9

IT IS an understatement to say that the spring of 1862 was a rainy time in Virginia. Rain fell week after week, month after month, until the country was neither land nor water but a soupy mixture of both. The last vestige of handsome uniforms disappeared, even among the natty legionnaires. Everything was the color of mud, everything had the feel of mud, everything tasted of mud. The tents and huts provided shelter when occupied, but an army cannot stay indoors because the weather is unkind. Drilling, scouting, picket duty and the constant bringing up of supplies went on as usual while the men cursed the elements, the Yankees and their own quartermaster department that could not or would not supply a change of clothing. The cavalry fared better by reason of its raids on Federal camps and baggage trains. These yielded welcome booty, especially overcoats and rubber blankets. Johnny Rebs in Northern uniforms seemed incongruous, but gradually they became a natural part of the picture. Up and down the line, from private to general and back again, soldiers were learning the vast difference between the romantic theory and the sober practice of warfare.

Because Hampton was now a brigadier, with a command four times its former number, his staff was proportionately larger. Preston was one of the number and young Wade would soon be another, both as lieutenants. Ezra Todd and

Festival Jones were also attached to the headquarters force. They were still rated as privates, but they had special duties. With the informality he could use so pleasantly, the general told them, "You are not my official aides, you are my neighbors from back home whom I shall call on at any time of day or night."

"Holler and we'll come a splashin'," Fess promised.

"This cursed mud!" Hampton looked at his caked boots.

"Day of sunshine to bake it on and we'll be bulletproof."

"Like knights in armor," Ezra added.

"By the way"—Hampton turned to him—"Did you finish *Ivanhoe*?"

"No, sir, but what I read before they destroyed my book I have with me forever. They can't take it away, though they'd like to. One day I'll finish it."

The general shook his head in a puzzled way, but, "It is impossible to understand some people," was all he said.

Though Ezra was now semi-officially attached to headquarters he had no clear picture of the whole military situation. There was much talk of operations in the West, and the Army of Tennessee, and what Stonewall Jackson was doing in the Shenandoah Valley, but, as with most soldiers, the war was only as much as he could see of it. That much, to his inexperienced eye, was not good. Scouts and spies were unanimous in saying that the Union Army was growing rapidly, was splendidly trained and had no end of food and equipment. Those who went up in the captive balloon behind the Confederate lines said the country was thick with enemy troops and at night their campfires outnumbered the stars.

There must be a hundred thousand men over there, they thought, while Johnston had less than half that number.

The rain continued, the mud got deeper, more men fell sick. Early in March word went around that the army would back up to better positions. On the eighth of the month Hampton was ordered to begin the movement with his brigade. As Ezra rode back and forth with messages he saw the baggage trains assembling. It was not a cheerful sight for the horses were poor, the wagons too few, and the roads all but impassable for loaded vehicles. Teamsters shouted and cracked their whips and cursed, officers splashed about, so bogged down they could not get out of each other's way. Infantry, cavalry, and artillery churned the ground almost to a lather and would have set to fighting among themselves had they not been blessed with an unusual patience and sense of humor. The regimental bands were ordered out and helped less with their music than with the ludicrous appearance they made, standing in the rain, sinking in the mud, and producing discords, squawks and tootles that kept the listeners roaring. It was a black day; everything went wrong and everyone was blamed for it.

"Judas priest!" Fess grumbled, when he and Ezra happened to meet late in the afternoon. "Iffen we're goin' to have a war, why don't we have one? I enlisted to fight, not to make mud pies."

"There'll be fighting," Ezra said, scraping the mud from his horse's neck. "Preston says the plan is to fall back till we get McClellan where we want him, then attack."

"Wade Hampton nary hatched that one," Fess declared.

"Iffen he was boss man we'd have attacked long ago and *put* McClellan where we want him."

Better-informed soldiers than Festival Jones were privately of the same mind. A month later when enemy troops came up from the James River, threatened Johnston's flank and were completely routed by Hampton, the feeling grew that what the army needed was more of the old bear-hunter's technique and less interference from the "kid-glove boys" in Richmond.

Still the slow retreat continued, with only flickering rear guard action. McClellan followed, politely careful not to step on Johnston's heels, though his commander-in-chief, Abraham Lincoln, had repeatedly ordered him to do something with that splendid army. It was not until the last day of May, at a place called Seven Pines only five miles from Richmond, that McClellan finally gave the order to attack.

Ezra came out of sleep to a long roll on the drums. Saddling up, something he could now do quicker than Fess, he trotted through camp toward headquarters. It was raining, and the men had spent a miserable night. Even those who had tents were wet and cold, so the army was in fighting mood. Everywhere soldiers were slogging through the mud, carrying their weapons at all angles, while they slung on their canteens and cartridge boxes and wolfed handfuls of cold food.

"What's up?" Ezra asked Preston, who was coming out of his father's tent.

"Pickets all driven in. Looks like a big push by the Yanks." Preston mounted with a flourish and was gone.

General Hampton pushed aside the tent flap and stepped

out, glancing about at the weather. He was calm, but his eyes were eager.

"Please hand this to Colonel Folsom of the 19th Georgia." He gave Ezra a folded note.

"Yes, sir." Ezra took it, saluted, and was off.

"And this to Colonel McElroy of the 16th North Carolina," Hampton said to Fess who had ridden up.

"Yes, General." Fess put it in his cartridge box to keep it dry. "Think the blue-bellies're askin' for hot vittles?"

"There are indications of it, Fess," Hampton answered.

Guessing soon gave place to certainty. Scouts all along the line sent word that the Union army was advancing, a fact every man's ears verified as the rumble of artillery soon became continuous. The Confederates were outnumbered and outgunned, but at last the hated rain had befriended them. During the night it had swollen the Chickahominy River so it overflowed and split the Federal force. Three corps were penned up on the north side and only two corps on the south were in fighting position. When Johnston grasped this providential situation he sent part of his troops to hold the few bridges over the river and threw his main strength against the two corps. They were the same ones he had routed at Bull Run months before.

Hampton's brigade was assigned to the left flank, close to the raging river where the fighting would be hottest. Ezra was nervous, but the agonizing fear he had known in his first battle was not with him. A year of army life, surrounded by men dying of sickness and wounds, had hardened him toward death. It came to everyone, and during the years or seconds before it came life was all that mattered. Life was opportunity, the only time given a man to do his work and prove his worth. Make the most of it, fill it with acts and thoughts he was not ashamed of, and death would have nothing to crow about. Such was the philosophy Ezra had evolved for his own defense and it stood the test of battle.

Pushing into the woods along the river was like deliberately entering a nightmare. The trees were in full leaf, their branches drooping and dripping rain, and around their trunks the endless gray water lapped with a million tongues. Paths and roads and clearings could be traced only by their lack of undergrowth, never by a glimpse of the ground. Men and horses advanced at a walk, feeling their way, not knowing if at the next step the water would be ankle-deep or over their heads. Where there was a stagnant pool, its surface was wimpled by the repercussion of cannon back on solid ground. At first there was no rifle fire, for the lines had not yet come to grips, and the splashing of myriad feet was a strange sound in the forest.

Always at home in the woods, Hampton appeared quite undisturbed as he rode ahead with his staff. He remarked to Preston that this was something like the swamps on their Mississippi plantation where they used to hunt bear. As he spoke he felt a tug at his hat and, taking it off, saw a bullet hole in the crown.

"Not bad shooting considering the visibility," he said. He put the hat on his head and turned to his aides. "Find the regimental commanders and tell them we will form our line on the rising ground ahead and there await developments."

The wait was short, for the Federals were just beyond the ridge. Both sides wanted the strip of comparatively dry earth and used their bayonets trying to get it. When Ezra returned he found the legionnaires in possession, prone behind such cover as they could find. The bluecoats had dropped back a safe distance, but some of them lay on the slope where they had fallen. Hampton had dismounted and stood beside a tree, examining the field through a telescope. After a moment he handed the glass to Preston, walked a few paces down the hill, pulled out his white handkerchief and waved it over his head.

"Father!" Preston shouted. "What are you doing?"

Ezra gripped his pistol and held his breath. Up and down the line riflemen were leaning forward, their muddy faces puzzled. Firing stopped in the immediate area. A Union officer stepped out, cupped his hands and called, "What do you want up there?"

Hampton's big voice roared back, "Some of your men are badly wounded. I suggest that you pick them up. We will hold our fire."

That was what happened. Stretcher-bearers carried away the fallen men and when they had finished the Federal officer saluted Hampton. He returned the salute gravely and then up from the Union line came a ringing cheer: "Hip, hip, hooray for Johnny Reb!" The general waved his sword in acknowledgment and walked back up the hill. Presently the rifle fire was resumed.

From what Ezra could see of the battle, no one was getting anywhere. The artillery roared steadily in the distance but there was no telling what it was shooting at. The business of Hampton's brigade was to halt the enemy advance along the river; this was being done without much fighting, as the Federals had stopped short of a general engagement. The Confederates waited, wet, cold, hungry and profane. The general sent repeated inquiries to G. W. Smith, who commanded the left wing, always receiving the same reply—to hold his position until further orders. Hampton rode up and down the line on his brown horse, looking bigger than ever in the mist, chewing twigs that he broke from trees, and waiting, waiting.

Early in the afternoon there was a sudden change. The Federals found a bridge that had been swept away bodily. Tying it to the bank with ropes they got an entire corps and battery across the river. It was a daring piece of work and they followed it up with a grim charge through the woods. Smith sent Hampton's, Pettigrew's, and Hutton's brigades to meet them. The two lines met with fixed bayonets, fell back a few yards, and opened a furious fire.

Ezra thought the world was ending. The crash of thousands of rifles seemed enough to tear a man to pieces even if he escaped the bullets. And how could anyone escape? Mud and water leaped high and dropped in a solid sheet. Small trees were cut off, their riddled branches stretched wide like imploring hands. Larger trees splintered and crashed under the impact of cannon balls. Men in blue and in gray pitched forward, backward, sideways, making grotesque gestures. Some writhed and struggled on the ground, others lay still.

"Git behind a tree, you fool!" Fess yelled in Ezra's ear.

"They'll get us all anyway." The boy was too numb to be nervous.

"We'll give 'em as much as they give us. Git behind a tree."

Ezra obeyed automatically and then looked around with strange detachment as though he were already a spirit beyond earthly danger. Hampton was a few yards away, a smoking pistol in each hand. Smith and Hutton were riding toward him; Hutton dropped his reins and slumped to the ground. Ezra knew he was dead and it seemed quite natural that he should be. Those who continued to live were somehow defying the laws of nature. Smith rode up to Hampton and the two sat talking, while not thirty yards away the undergrowth was flashing with Union fire.

Preston cantered up and joined the two generals. More than ever he looked and acted like his father, except that he was smiling.

"They want to git hit," Fess raged. "Look at 'em bunch up so's even a blue-belly couldn't miss 'em."

"They'll get us all anyway," Ezra repeated dully.

"Shut up, you croakin' buzzard!" Fess slapped him in the face.

"Do that again and I'll mop the ground with you." Ezra's eyes blazed.

"Now you sound like a man."

"If you think— He's hit, Fess, he's hit!"

"Who's hit?"

"The general. Come on!"

Hampton sat straight in the saddle, but one foot was out of the stirrup, blood pouring through a hole in the boot.

"You should go to the rear, sir!" Smith leaned over and shouted.

"No, no! I can still ride." Hampton waved him back.

"But the blood, sir." Smith motioned to Preston. "Lieutenant, ride to the field hospital at the forks of the road and fetch Dr. Gaillard."

"Yes, sir."

"I must be off, Hampton. Pettigrew is wounded and needs support. Your men are holding splendidly." Smith galloped away.

"We'll stand in front of the general so them heathens can't see he's hit," Fess said in Ezra's ear. They reined their horses ahead of the big brown hunter.

Minié balls whistled and shells screamed while the two lines stood there toe to toe, shooting each other to ribbons. Preston and Dr. Gaillard galloped up. A bullet dropped the doctor's horse and the surgeon rolled in the mud, but he picked himself up, kit and all, and smiled at Hampton.

"Please dismount for an examination, General."

"And risk not being able to mount again, Doctor?"

"Then put out your foot."

Hampton thrust out a leg that was as hard as a tree trunk. Preston pulled off the long boot. The doctor went after the bullet with a knife and a probe, while the general chewed his mustache and pretended to watch the battle. The foot was bandaged, the boot replaced and everyone went back to the fight—a mere incident on that field of blood.

The afternoon dragged on, awful hours of rain and suffering and death among the trees and in the water. Reports came in that Longstreet had failed to break the Union line south of the river. Then Johnston was badly wounded and Smith took command. Hampton held, but he paid a terrific price; half his men were casualties, though not one was a prisoner.

Darkness crept into the forest and across the clearings and gradually the firing died out. One of the last shots toppled Ezra from his horse.

Chapter 10

EZRA did not black out. He felt as though he had been knocked from his saddle by an unseen fist and he lay for a few seconds, fighting to get his wind back. Then he knew he had been hit by a bullet in the right shoulder. It burned, began to ache, and soon his whole arm and hand was one throbbing pain. He felt the wound and found it bleeding freely, the warm, sticky wetness spreading over his ribs with sickening rapidity.

Unlike some of the soldiers, he had scoffed at the idea of carrying a bottle of iodine or ammonia for such an emergency. But he did have a large handkerchief, one of those sent out by the women of Richmond before linen became scarce. He got it out and stuffed it into the bullet hole as he might have plugged a leaking boat. After a while the bleeding was less, but the pain had spread to his finger tips. He imagined it was expanding like something solid that would eventually explode.

By then night had come. Gunfire had ceased and its place was taken by worse sounds. The black field was casting up the cries of the wounded. Boys from North and South, suffering and frightened, were calling on God and man for help. They spoke the same language and begged for the same mercy. "Water!" "In the name of Christ give me a drink!"

"Help me or I'll bleed to death!" "My guts are out—for God's sake shoot me!"

To escape the clammy fingers of the mud Ezra sat with his back against a tree and tried to think. He knew he could walk and should find a dressing station, but an indescribable weariness was upon him—the hopeless, despondent fatigue that follows battle. He neither knew nor cared how the fight had gone. If he had heard that the war was over it would have made little difference then. Nothing mattered except his own pain and exhaustion. The screams of agony about him were not disturbing; they were merely natural sounds in those surroundings, the inevitable accompaniment to war.

Lights began showing on the field, round eyes of bull's-eye lanterns and flickering flames of candles, as searchers from both sides moved in to pick up the wounded. At sight of them the cries increased. Ezra knew he was still losing some blood and should have attention. In spite of the pain it was easier to sit there and—and what? Die in the mud like a stricken frog? Men didn't do that unless they were unable to struggle.

A light shone in his face and a voice asked, "Need help, Johnny?"

"You wouldn't help me, Yank." Ezra came out of his languor and spoke defiantly.

"Don't be such a fool. Where are you hit?"

"Shoulder. I can walk."

"Better be moving then. Try your legs while I'm here to steady you."

Ezra got slowly to his feet, wondering why he obeyed an

enemy he did not fear. Who said they were enemies? Men in Washington and Richmond who had never seen a battle-field at night or felt the bond of mutual misery.

"Thanks, Yank," he said humbly. "I can make it now."

"All right, Johnny. Say, my canteen is empty and the boys are hollering for water. Is there a stream hereabouts?"

"I don't know. Take my canteen; it's half full."

"You're a white man, Johnny. Good luck to you!"

"Same to you, Yank."

Ezra went slowly up the ridge that seemed miles high. Stumps, fallen trees, and human bodies tripped him, but he kept on. The number of wounded decreased, for most of them had been evacuated that far back. The night was comparatively quiet except for the occasional terrific groan of a dying horse. Suddenly the way became smooth, and Ezra's feet told him he was in a road. Roads led somewhere, else they would not be roads. He tried to remember where this one went, but his head felt light. Strange it should be light when the rest of him was so heavy. He planted his legs wide apart to steady himself and was aware that the warm wet feeling now reached to his foot. That shoulder was at it again. Perhaps if he sat down for a while—

"Whoa!" A lantern with a voice came out of his sleep and he resented being disturbed. "Don't run over the man."

"Hi, Yank," Ezra said drowsily.

"I ain't no Yank," the lantern said. "You hurted?"

"Yes."

"Got room fer one more in the am'blance. Want a lift?"

"Sure." Ezra stood up and found he was not two feet from a span of mules. "Two-wheeler or four?"

"Four. Them two-wheeler dumpcarts ain't fitten to put wounded inter—heads up one minute, heels up next. Come on, git in. Feller jest died on us 'n' we hove him out. You take his place."

"I can ride on the seat. Save the shelf for somebody worse hurt."

"Suit yourself."

The seat, when Ezra finally climbed up to it, was a bare board. The ambulance, which was without springs, was a cupboard on wheels with tiers of shelves for the wounded. Sometimes men smothered in there, or hemorrhaged to death as a result of the jolting, which mattered not at all to the drivers who were as callous as gravediggers. They had to be, a sensitive man would have gone mad listening to the screams, groans, prayers and curses.

"For heaven's sake! Can't you be more careful?" Ezra cried, as the wagon lurched into a hole. "You're killing those boys back there."

"Aw, shut up," the driver growled. "I can't see the road."

"One of you might walk ahead with a lantern."

"We ain't walkin' fer nobody," the second man said. "If you think this is rough, you oughter see the wounded shipped to Richmond—dumped into hoss cars that ain't been cleaned out sence the hosses was in 'em."

"It's a crime." Ezra clutched the side of the swaying wagon.

"What the hell do you expect? This is war, ain't it?"

"Yes, but—"

"Shut up!" the driver roared. " 'N' stay shut up lessen you want to be throwed out."

Ezra hung onto the seat silently, trying to concentrate on the thought that they would reach the hospital soon and things would be better. Finally they did reach it. It was a plantation that had been taken over by the doctors, not only the house itself but the stables, slave quarters, sheds and poultry houses. Every bit of shelter from the rain was full of wounded and more were pouring in. In the blackness it looked like a small village illuminated by scores of lanterns for a celebration. But it was a macabre party, with music of groans and dancing to measures of agony.

Ezra slid from the ambulance and walked unsteadily toward what might have been a hay barn. Its wide door was open and three lanterns hanging from a beam just inside threw an almost cheerful glow outward. Beside the door was what his careless glance took for a pile of firewood. He stepped aside to let some stretcher-bearers pass. An orderly was in the doorway swinging a human arm as casually as though it were a dead cat. Then he threw it on the pile and went back. The whole heap was arms, legs, feet and hands.

Feeling sick, Ezra leaned against the barn, then inched along and rested his sound shoulder against the frame of an open window. The wounded of both armies covered the barn floor, which was littered with hay. They lay and sat and stood in all positions, according to the nature of their wounds. Those who had been brought in early were bandaged and put away under blankets at the far end of the room, where some of the lesser wounded were passing out water and swinging cedar branches at swarms of flies and mosquitoes. Progressively toward the door the casualties had received less and less attention. The latest arrivals were caked with mud and blood. Leaves, twigs and pine needles were still sticking to them, as they had been picked up on the field. In one corner was a table made of fence boards, where the red-armed surgeons were working on a naked figure that lay still in the lantern light. Everywhere the wounded men who were conscious were watching, watching, reaching out with their eyes for someone to help them.

Ezra covered his face with his good hand, but there was little escape in that. A sickening smell was in the air and every breath seemed to fill his stomach instead of his lungs. Throughout the barn were sounds of pain and fear from boys who a few hours before had laughed as they went into battle. Now they were broken, no longer vainglorious warriors but common little humans from farms and shops and schoolrooms who cried to be spared the bitter cup. Too shattered to speak coherently, they repeated some word over and over—"God, God, God"—"Mother, mother." Those with abdominal wounds lay silent until the paroxysms came, then screamed, and tore at anything their hands could reach. The unconscious ones groaned with every breath. One was laughing in happy delirium. Misery everywhere—too much of it— more than a man could stand. Ezra leaned through the window, thinking his time had come and dimly thankful for it.

Thirst awakened him. It was no casual wish to drink, but a maddening desire for water. "Water!" he shouted before he knew where he was. "Water! Water!"

"Comin', brother, comin'," a weary voice answered.

"Hurry up! Where are you?"

"Yes, yes, yes. I've lugged enough water in the past twelve hours to fill Chesapeake Bay." A big man with a black beard and red-rimmed eyes seemed to lean out of the sky. "Wait till I help you set up. There, now drink till you bust." He held a tin dipperful of water to Ezra's lips.

As he drank Ezra looked over the edge of the dipper and saw he was in a corner of the barn floor. "Thank you," he said when the water was gone. "How did I get here?"

"You was lucky," Black Beard said. "They dug out the ball 'fore you come to."

"I must have fainted." Ezra noticed that his shoulder was bandaged.

"Mebbe you died. I ain't sure this ain't the hereafter they warned us agin." The man limped away on flat, aching feet.

Ezra rested on one elbow and looked at the man beside him, a youngster with the waxen face of death. The blanket that covered him dropped away sharply at the knees, showing that both legs were gone. Ezra shuddered. A bullet in the shoulder seemed a small thing. Still, it was enough to make him feel sick. He lay down and listened to Bedlam.

Somehow the night passed and with it went many of the soldiers in the barn, among them the boy next to Ezra. A letter in his pocket showed he was from Michigan and Black Beard volunteered to write to his family. When daylight dimmed the lanterns the flies increased. To escape them the surgeons moved their table outdoors where a stiff wind was blowing. The wounded lay under a buzzing cloud and moaned for protection more than for water. Men of the hospital service, who had been on their feet all day and all night, stumbled back and forth, swinging evergreen branches, too weary to curse the flies. But such wounded as could talk supplied that deficiency.

The pain in his shoulder was less than Ezra had expected, but the loss of blood made him sick and weak. He dozed in the early morning, then awoke and tried to sit up, getting only as far as his elbow again.

"May I help you?" Ezra looked up and saw that the Michigan's boy's place had been taken by another Yankee who was sitting up. He was a captain, perhaps forty years old. "My arms are O. K. and at your service."

"I can't make it." Ezra lay down. "Thanks, Yank."

"When I enlisted they didn't tell me my worst enemies would be flies," the captain said in a patient, good-humored voice that belied his haggard face. "You been in long?"

"Since it started."

"A fellow gets to think a lot between battles, doesn't he?"

"You're plumb right, Yank. They say we're brave to go into battle, but they don't say, because they don't know, that we need ten times as much courage when the battle's over and we have time to think about it."

"You seem to have thought things out thoroughly, for a youngster." The captain looked at him with deep, keen eyes.

"And a rebel," Ezra shot back.

"We are all rebels," the Northerner said quietly. "If we hadn't rebelled at something none of us would be here."

"That's something to chew on." Ezra looked closer at the other's long, thoughtful face. "But where'd you go to school that you wasn't learned that down here we're all rebels to be hated?"

"Oh, they taught us that—or tried to." The captain smiled slowly. "At first we thought we did hate you, then we suffered the same things you suffered, we shared pain and death with you—and we lost our hatred."

"Well, I'll be darned!" Ezra stared at the man. "I never heard a Yank talk that way before. Do you mean you ain't my enemy?"

"Oh!" The captain moved a leg under the blanket, winced, then smiled. "Technically I am, but not personally. I would fight you again, not because I want your blood but because I want to end the war and live in peace."

After a minute of thought Ezra looked into the steady blue eyes across from him and said, "Of all the tomfool reasoning on both sides! You and I and lots of others want to be friends, but instead of being friends and pleasuring in it we light out and try to kill one another."

"Johnny," the captain said warmly, "we seem to think along the same lines. After the war we should get together and discuss numerous things."

"I guess we'll have time to do some of it now," Ezra said ruefully. "Though I ain't got the veezum to talk much."

"I won't be here long," the captain said. "I have only a flesh

wound in the leg so they will soon move me to a prison camp.
But after the war. What is your name?"

"Ezra Todd."

"Ezra Todd!"

"Sure. What's so queer about that?"

"Nothing, only—"

"Listen!"

A high-pitched voice cut cheerfully through the medley of depressing sounds: "Wake up and sing, you birds, here comes your breakfast. Hot soup, *hot* soup, hot *soup* fer ever'-body. Blue-bellied Yanks 'n' Johnny Rebs, here's somethin' to lay the dust in Johnnycake Lane 'n' make you praise the Lord till the cows come home. Set up iffen you can, but iffen you can't I'll slop it inter you. Yes sir, here I be— Hog it down— Don't mention it, Yank. Us Johnnies aim ter give our visiters their bellies full—hot lead, hot soup, take yer choice— Eh? You don't want none, mister? Judas priest! Then I'll feed it to my dog. Here, Spot, here!"

"Fess!" Ezra yelled as loud as he could and tried to sit up

"Comin', brother, soup train stops at your station in a jiffy."

"It's me—Ezra."

"I'll be a billy goat!" Fess stepped over a line of wounded and dropped to his knees beside Ezra. "I didn't know you was here, bub. Bad hit?"

"Shoulder. You got it too?" For Fess' head was bandaged.

"Sculp wound. Have some soup?"

"Sure. I don't remember when I ate last. Guess I can't sit up."

"Let's have your paw. Easy. So! Can you balance?"

"I guess so."

"Here's the bellywash."

"Give the other dipper to the Yank there. He's hungry too."

"Yeh. Have all you want, they're makin' it in caldron kittles."

Ezra drank and the warm liquid made him tingle.

"What are you doing here, Fess?" he finally asked.

"They're short-handed, so I offered to help."

"What about the battle and the general?"

"Dunno. I've got to git along now, the boys need me. I'll be back, bub. 'Nother round, Yank?"

"No, thank you." The captain handed him the dipper. "I appreciate your kindness."

"As a rule, we murder our prisoners, but we hain't got time today. See you later." Fess moved away, pail, dippers and tongue all rattling.

"Are you too tired to talk, Todd?" the captain asked in a low voice.

"No, I feel better now."

"Then do you mind telling me where you got your name?"

"Where I got it? Why, I suppose my folks gave it to me."

"Do you know their names?"

"Sure. Cyrus and Alice Todd."

"Was your mother's maiden name Marsh?"

"Yes. How do you know?"

"Ezra"—the captain's eyes burned into him—"I am your uncle."

"The deuce!" Ezra got up on his elbow again. "Who are you?"

"George Marsh from New York. Did you ever hear that name before?"

"Not that I remember." Ezra stared hard at him. "I was pretty young when my parents died and the neighbors who raised me wouldn't know. Are you—are you sure about it?"

"It must be true, Ezra."

"Say!" Ezra felt suddenly weaker than ever and lay down. "It is *something* if I have found my family!"

"Even if they are Yanks?" Captain Marsh smiled that slow smile of his.

"Oh, I always knew that much. Father was a schoolmaster and came down here for his health."

"By jinks!" The captain slapped his sound leg. "Both ends of the story match perfectly."

"Not quite." Ezra was thinking fast. "If my mother was your sister, how come you didn't know what became of her?"

"You have a right to ask that—and I have a right to be ashamed to answer it, Ezra." Marsh picked at his blanket a moment. "The trouble started with my father—your grandfather. He was a business fanatic. He thought only business men were of any account in this world. Your father was different—scholarly, dreamy. Father forbade your mother to marry him, but she did. Your grandfather disowned her. This is what I am ashamed of—I allowed myself to lose track of her. Did she ever speak of me?"

"Not that I remember. Or of my grandfather."

"But she must have forgiven him, for she gave you his name."

"Is he dead?"

"Yes."

"Then there's nothing to be done about it."

"Nothing they can do about it. But possibly I can make some atonement. You and I, Ezra, can start from here and mend the family break."

"We can't do much mending when the war makes us enemies."

"We aren't really enemies, are we, Ezra?"

"Well, you're a Yank and I'm a Johnny Reb. And I'm going to stay one, in case you're hinting that I turn my coat."

"No, no, no, young rooster. What I mean is, we are both Americans—that is bigger than either side."

"Golly, that's a tall way to look at it."

"It's the only way to look at it, Ezra."

Ezra felt strangely happy and contented. "I didn't know you Yanks felt that way," he said. "I thought you wanted to wipe us out."

"Some of us do," Marsh said, "the same as some Southerners prefer death to union."

Ezra was up on his elbow once more. "All to once I have a family! Mister man, what it's worth just to know that!" He lay down quickly and turned his head.

The captain gave no sign of noticing his emotion and, after a while, asked casually, "What are your plans when the war is over?"

"I haven't got that far."

"What about the people you were living with?"

Ezra told him that story, sweating and panting with weakness.

"I take it General Hampton is your hero," Marsh commented.

"Yes, sir, he is. I'd sure enough die for that man."

"You have your own future to map out. Even as worthy a man as Hampton should not dominate you, especially after the war."

"Oh, I'll find something to do, if I pull through."

"Not just 'something,' Ezra, something constructive. After these years of destruction the nation will need builders more than ever. Did you ever think of railroading as a business?"

"Heck, no! I don't know anything about railroads. Do you?"

"It is my business."

"You run trains?" Ezra was interested.

"I have, but I am more concerned with building railroads. It is a great business and after the war it will increase a thousandfold as we push the roads across the continent."

"You mean *way* across?"

"Yes, to California and all the intervening country. Millions of acres will be opened to settlement and their minerals, lumber, foodstuffs and manufactured goods given access to world markets. Railroads will create the mightiest nation this world has ever seen. Would you like to have a hand in it?"

"Golly!" Ezra breathed faster. "I never thought of such a thing."

"Think it over. This war is only an incident in history.

Beyond it are greater things waiting to be done. Perhaps we can do our part of some of them together. If that appeals to you, look me up in New York."

"Thank you, sir—er, Uncle George." Ezra spoke the last two words slowly as though they tasted good.

The captain glanced toward the door and leaned over to shake hands. "They are coming for me," he said cheerfully. "I will write my family about this so, in case something happens to me, you may have a haven in the home port if you ever want it."

"I—I am mighty glad I met you, Uncle George," was all Ezra could think of to say.

"Captain Marsh?" A soldier carrying a crutch stopped beside them.

"Right." The captain moved to stand up.

"Your hand, Yank." The soldier reached down. "That's it. Now lean on this stick."

"Thank you, Johnny." The captain looked back and smiled, then hobbled away.

For a while after that, Ezra forgot himself and his surroundings. It was all but overwhelming suddenly to find that he was not alone in the world, but was one of a family. He knew little enough about that family, yet it existed, it was his, he had relatives the same as other people had. He felt like shouting for all the world to come and see that he was not a wind-blown leaf but part of a living tree. A real somebody with a future. The captain's calm view of things was so different from what Ezra had known that he seemed to be breathing a new kind of titillating atmosphere. It was such a new conception of life, so vast and so full of possibilities, that his weakened body and mind fell asleep trying to explore it.

He awoke dripping sweat and sharply aware of his discomfort. He cursed the luck that kept him there amid the heat and flies and broken men, but he could not muster enough strength to crawl away. He had a fierce longing to be out in the woods, where the air was sweet and cool and quiet, with birds overhead and pine needles for a bed, where he could think. There was so much to think about now, so many ideas that were different and must be handled in a new way. How could a country boy get well without even a tree to look at? Yet the hospital people were doing their best and he should be thankful to be alive.

The vacant place beside him was soon given to a big fellow who had been burned in a powder explosion. In his delirium he kept shouting he was from Alabamy and could lick Abe Lincoln. He died about noon and Fess helped carry him out.

Fess was everywhere, fetching water and food, smoothing blankets, rubbing cramped muscles, fighting flies, and listening to boys who had to talk to someone. If it is possible to imagine a bowlegged angel in ragged trousers and shirt, with a long, dirty face and ears covered with yellow hair, that was Festival Jones.

"Bub," he confided to Ezra that night, "I'm so plumb tuckered out I could sleep in a briar patch."

"You will have a chance to sleep tonight."

"With all these fellers to play mammy to?"

"Tomorrow then."

"Tomorrer I go to Richmond to find out what's happened to the gen'ral. Nobody knows nothin' here."

"The general will be taken care of."

"I want to know!" Fess sighed. "Anything I can do fer you, bub?"

Ezra thought of telling him about Captain Marsh, but they were both too weary. Besides, it was not good policy to be overheard boasting about Yankee relatives.

"Get me out of here, Fess," he begged. "I'll die in this hole. Drag me out under the trees."

"Mebbe they'll shift you to Richmond."

"That's sure death! You've heard what those hospitals are."

"Yeh, they hain't exactly a promise of long life."

"I'm from the country, Fess." Ezra was sobbing in spite of himself. "I'll die in one of those city deathtraps. Drag me out under the trees."

"Tell you what," Fess said soothingly, "you be good 'n' keep quiet 'n' let the doctors tinker you up till I git back from Richmond 'n' I'll git you outen here."

"When will you be back?"

"Two—three days. You can tough it out that long."

"If you promise."

"Shore, I promise, bub."

"And, Fess, thanks for what you've done for me today."

"Want I should kiss you good night?"

"Get out of here, you old porcupine!"

"Feelin' better already." There was relief in Fess' voice. "See you later, bub."

Chapter 11

LYING there in the barn, swarmed over by flies, pestered by vermin, and surrounded by suffering men, Ezra set himself to "tough it out," as the soldiers put it. There was more to think about now, which helped when he was in a thinking mood. New vistas of his past and future combined to make the present more endurable.

His pain was severe, but it annoyed him less than his physical weakness. To be unable to raise his head from the floor without feeling the earth spin like a leaf in a whirlpool made him furious with himself. When the doctor dressed his wound he demanded medicine that would get him out in a hurry.

"Time is the only medicine for you," the surgeon mumbled, holding a bandage in his teeth.

"How much time?"

"Perhaps a month."

"I'll die in this place before a month is up."

"That may be." The doctor seemed unconcerned as he applied the bandage. "I will try to transfer you to Richmond in two or three days."

Ezra said nothing more. He thought of the suffocating boxcars and other things he had heard about the care of the wounded. The Confederacy was doing its best, but the sudden needs of tens of thousands of sick and injured men were beyond its resources. Doctors were never numerous in the

South and now, with a shortage of supplies due to the blockade, they were working at a fearful disadvantage. Hospitals, not battlefields, were feared above all other places.

For these reasons Richmond was a greater threat to Ezra's peace of mind than McClellan's Army of the Potomac. By the way, he thought, what had become of that army? The sound of guns had faded out, but no one who came to the barn was sure why. Rumors were as persistent as the flies: Johnston was dead and the Confederates in rout, McClellan was a prisoner in Richmond, the Federals were in full retreat, both armies were exhausted and holding their same positions, Abraham Lincoln had arrived during the battle and, being drunk as usual, had fallen off his horse and broken a leg or two, or Jefferson Davis had been struck by lightning.

The next day Ezra tried a dozen times before he managed to sit up alone. He propped himself against the wall and hung on, trembling and oozing sweat. Looking out across the barn floor he counted two hundred and nine wounded men in every imaginable position. Those who could move were twisting and turning, trying to relieve aching muscles, striking at flies, reaching for water buckets. Some struggled deliriously, others lay in coma, a few were playing cards. All had the rumpled, dirty look of sick people who are uncared for. Innumerable smells had combined to form an indescribable stink; the air was so thick it seemed almost possible to cut it in chunks and throw it out the windows. Ezra gasped and slid down full length on the floor. "Dear Lord," he prayed silently, "get me out of here. I don't want to die, so please get me out of here."

The visible answer to that prayer was Festival Jones. He came rolling in on his bowlegs, carrying a double armful of cigars tied in bundles with red ribbon. They were, he said, loot from a Federal camp, but the truth was he had bought them in the city with his last dollars. When he had distributed them to Johnnies and Yanks alike he squatted on his heels beside Ezra and offered him one of the ribbons for a necktie.

"Hang it on that nail in the wall," Ezra said. "It will be something bright to look at."

"When I'm gone."

"What tells you you're bright to look at?"

"Any lookin' glass."

"Huh. What's the news in Richmond? How is the general?"

"Sent home—his foot."

"Is it bad?"

"No."

"Sure?"

"Got it from young Wade. He's on his father's staff."

"Where is the legion?"

"Outside Richmond with the rest of the army."

"We got licked?"

"No. The blue-bellies're fallin' back but we hain't in rig to foller 'em." Fess twisted the ribbon. "We lost pretty heavy. Robert E. Lee's in command now."

"He's the one from Virginia we've heard about?"

"Yeh." Fess lowered his voice. "Young Wade says it hain't out yet, but Lee's goin' to slap all the cavalry together in one lump 'n' use it independent of the rest of the army. No more of this piddlin' 'round with the infantry—we'll fight man-fashion."

"I'll never fight again if I stay here much longer, Fess."

"Can you walk, bub?"

"I don't think so."

"Then I'll lug you. I've got orders to transfer you." He gave Ezra a warning look. "Pack your trunk and we'll git goin'."

"Give me a hand. I'll try to walk."

When Ezra got to his feet, the floor seemed so far below that he felt dizzy. His head wanted to float away, his knees tried to bend, and the effort of holding himself erect made the sweat run down his back. He put an arm around Fess' neck and they made the long march to the door. It was tough going, but worth it when he looked out at the sky, the trees and the green fields.

"Do you have permission to leave?" A hospital orderly popped up in the doorway.

"Sonny," Fess told him, "my name is Festival Jones and this is Ez Todd. Write it down in case you're handy at dis-rememberin'. Iffen you want our pedigrees ask Gen'ral Hampton. Likewise, should you hold us up and this feller dies on your hands you'll settle with the gen'ral—or he'll settle with you."

"Where are you going?" the orderly demanded.

"To jine the gen'ral in South Caroliny, iffen we live that long. Now git outten the way 'fore this boy kerflummoxes."

Fess picked Ezra up and carried him across the yard. A span of mules hitched to a light wagon stood under a tree. He laid Ezra on some blankets in the wagon bed, climbed to the seat, and drove away. Before turning into the main road he stopped and twisted around.

"How you ridin', bub?"

"Good. But we aren't headed for South Carolina, are we?"

"Not direct, but mebbe some time when the war's over we'll jine the gen'ral there."

"Where are we going now?"

"Dunno. We'll find a quiet place to lay up."

"You aren't on leave, are you?"

"I'm wounded. Can't you see the bandage on my head?"

"I don't believe—"

"Hush up! Mind iffen Spot rides back there with you?"

"No," Ezra smiled.

"All right, Spot, hop in. Don't wallopse 'round 'n' hurt the man's sore shoulder." Fess clucked to the mules and turned them down the road.

Ezra lay back and looked up at the sky, which was cloudless for the first time in weeks. The sunshine caressed him and the soft air of late spring filled his lungs and went singing through his blood. There was not a fly in sight, not a groan or a sob to be heard, not a smell that did not come from healthy living things. He knew by the sound that traffic was heavy on the road, but he did not raise his head to see it. Though the bumping of the wagon hurt his shoulder, it was the pain of motion, not the dull ache of inaction, and so less disturbing. For the moment, the world was a pleasant place and he fell asleep.

When the wagon wheels stopped turning he awoke. Pine trees were talking with a breeze and between him and the sky a score of vultures were sailing round and round.

"Where are we, Fess?" he asked drowsily.

"Dunno." Fess was climbing down over a wheel. "I took the first shun-pike I come to 'n' kept goin'. Told my team to go where they'd a mind to."

"*Your* team?"

"Yeh. Found 'em hitched to a tree. Looked all over 'n' couldn't find the owner."

"You old crook!"

"That hain't a nice way to talk, bub. This rig is a army rig—belongs to Jeff Davis. I went all over, behind trees 'n' fences 'n' in the woods, hollerin', 'Mister Davis, *Mister* Davis, Mister *Davis*,' but I couldn't git a peep outen him. So I took the team to save 'em from standin' there in the sun 'n' mebbe gittin' sunburned. 'Where you goin' with them gov'ment mules?' a soldier says to me. " 'Goin' to move two wounded men of Hampton's Legion,' I says to him. 'Go ahead,' he says."

"I wouldn't wonder if you finally got out of this world alive." Ezra laughed for the first time in days.

"Dry, be you?"

"Yes. Got some water?"

"Yeh. Also grub, rifles, ammunition, ever'thing fer a nice little vacation trip."

"You found them too, I suppose."

"Yeh. Help you set up?"

"I can make it."

Ezra sat up and leaned against the wagon seat, taking a long drink from the canteen Fess handed him. Then he looked around curiously. A few days before the place had been a forest, but now only a few pines were left standing. The rest was a littered dump: broken wagons, dead horses, muskets, haversacks, parts of uniforms—everything that soldiers could discard in a hurry. Crisscrossing among the stumps and splintered trees was a tangle of rutted wagon tracks thick as wrinkles on an old face. Vultures by the hundred were flopping and squawking, too busy with their vile banquet to be afraid.

"Let's get out of here," Ezra said wearily. "I'm tired and sick of destruction."

"You hain't fixin' to quit the war, bub?"

"Listen, Fess," Ezra said, defiant with weariness, "I can quit if I want to and have a place to go. I could walk out of this army, when I am able to walk, and go to New York and stay with my family." He told him about Captain Marsh. "What do you think of that?"

"Well"—Fess rubbed his chin—"as you allus knowed your kin was from the North, what's so surprisin' to find yourself related to Yanks?"

"Oh, can't you see? Can't you understand? It doesn't matter that they're Yanks—it's that I've found a family that wants me!"

"Yeh, yeh, that's a heap." Fess nodded. "Too bad you 'n' your kin're on dif'rent sides of the fence."

"That won't make any odds in the long run, Fess. When the war is over, North and South will be one again and ten times bigger than before."

"You sort of take the Yankee slant," Fess observed mildly.

"Well," Ezra paused. "I don't know what's going to happen, but things will work out. Come west with me and you'll see."

"I hain't goin' west," Fess answered firmly. "I don't want no railroad or no gold mine or no cow farm. I don't want nothin' but my little place up in Cashier's Valley. I'm goin' to spend my days there—after I've fit out this war."

"I'm going to fight it out too, but I hate it. The whole thing makes me sick. Take me away from here, Fess." Tears smarted in the boy's eyes.

"Shore, bub. We'll take us a vacation. Iffen they can't fight the war without us, they'll have to let it set till we git back."

Fess climbed onto the seat and steered the team into an area that had not been desolated. The battle had swept by like a storm and its edge was visible for miles. Wreckage was on one side, unblemished country on the other. The road entered pine woods where the wagon wheels rolled softly in sandy ruts.

"We'll bait in this clearin'," Fess decided. Then he added, "I guess not, though, it's a graveyard."

Ezra looked over the side and saw rows of fresh pine slabs with names and dates inscribed with a hot iron, each marking a grave. The mounds were freshly sodded and the plot was surrounded by a log fence.

"New Englanders," Fess commented. "They fuss with their graveyards."

"Neat people," Ezra muttered, remembering the flower beds and pebbled walks his parents tended. "Good people—and we are killing them."

"They're killin' us too, bub. It's root, hog, or die."

"I know—I know." Ezra lay down in the wagon.

They went on through the afternoon with no destination in mind except to get away from the battle lines. It was a country of woods and farms, a pleasant landscape as yet untouched by war. But war had hit the people. There were no young men to be seen and most of the Negroes had run after the Union Army. Only a few old folks of both races were keeping an eye on things, pretending in a feeble, pathetic way to protect their homes and livestock from marauders in blue or gray. They stood at their gates displaying the white flag of neutrality and, when they saw that the approaching dust was not raised by the expected columns but by a wagon bearing a wounded man, they offered water and corn bread and begged for news.

In the evening Fess pulled up beside a stream and made camp. Aside from the mosquitoes, it was a peaceful spot without a sound except the moving water and a nightingale's voice.

"How 'bout some bread 'n' bacon?" Fess sang out.

"That's better than hospital soup," Ezra said. "Why do they feed sick men that bellywash?"

"Food hain't plenty like it was. Lots of talk in Richmond."

"Oh, talk, talk, talk!" Ezra swayed and caught hold of a

wagon wheel. "Everybody talks and nobody knows what they're talking about. Isn't there anybody on earth who can shut up and think?"

"You're all tuckered out," Fess said patiently. "I'll fix a blanket 'n' you lay down."

After a while Ezra nibbled at the greasy food and fell to watching the stars. The hospital and its horrors was behind him. That was something. What now? Was he going to live or die? At the moment he didn't much care which way it went. Buck up, Johnny Reb. *Fortes fortuna juvat.* Tonight he was too tired to set his teeth into that, but tomorrow— Thank heaven there was always a tomorrow.

Before starting out in the morning Fess washed Ezra's shoulder with spring water and put a clean bandage on it. He said the wound was healing well; this did not make sense to the boy who felt as sick and weak as ever.

"Leave me beside the road and go back to the army," he said gloomily. "You enlisted to fight, not to nursemaid me.

"Have fit 'n' aim to fight again after I've had a breather," Fess answered.

"You can't just walk out when you feel like it."

"Thousands're doin' it. 'Sides, I'm wounded."

"That is only a scratch on your head. You're playing pos͘ sum as an excuse to take care of me."

"Hush your mouth, wind-head, we're movin'.'"

"The faster the better."

"Spot's runnin' a rabbit in the woods, but he'll pick up our track. I nary seen a sharper nose'n hisn."

The mules poked along at their own pace, keeping to by-

ways through a country of covered bridges and rolling farmlands. Everywhere the people were nervous and apprehen-
sive, friendly at heart but afraid that even two wounded men
might betray them to foragers.

In the afternoon they came to a stone house that, even at a
distance, had a cordial atmosphere. A tall man in a wide-
brimmed hat and square-cut clothes stood by the gate under a
tulip tree and smiled when they stopped.

"Mister," Fess addressed him, "we're in a pucker for water.
Can we git some here?"

"Yes, friend, or milk if thee prefers it." The man's voice
was deep and soft.

"Milk!" Ezra sat up in the wagon. "That sounds good."

"Thee are sick, friend?"

"Wounded. You are a Quaker?"

"Yes. Yonder is the dairy house." The man nodded toward
a small stone building, an unusual one for those parts.

Fess drove the mules to it and stopped by the open door.
A spring bubbled inside and ran away over slabs of cool stone.
On them sat perhaps two dozen earthen bowls full of milk
under thick covers of wrinkled cream. From pegs in the wall
hung wooden skimming spoons, gourds of various sizes and
a tin cup.

The Quaker poised the cup and said to Ezra, "Cream if
thee wishes, but thee will find it rich for a sick stomach."

"Milk is all right," Ezra said. "We are beggars, you know,
and have no money to buy what we choose."

"Take a gourd and help thyself," the man directed Fess, as
he filled the cup.

They drank slowly in long, cool swallows.

"Mister," Fess said heartily, "I've heard of the milk of human kindness, but this is the first time I ever really met up with it."

The man smiled. "Thee did not expect me to refuse a friend?"

"But we're soldiers 'n' you're agin fightin'."

"I am not against those who fight."

"You hain't on neither side in this war?"

"To me there are no sides. The nation is one in its misunderstanding."

"That's somethin' to chew on," Fess said in a puzzled tone. He looked through the doorway at Ezra. "What do you think, bub?"

"I think this is the place we are looking for, Fess."

"Mister," Fess said abruptly, halting the gourd halfway to his mouth, "iffen you'll let us lay up here till the boy gits back on his pins, I'll work for you and when we go I'll give you this span of mules."

"Thee are welcome to stay without pay." And plainly he meant it.

"Not by a jugful!" Fess emptied the gourd and smacked approvingly. "You're one in a million, but we hain't passin' the hat. Do we stay or do we start huntin' for somebody who hain't kin to the Good Samaritan?"

"Stay on thy own terms," the Quaker answered reluctantly as though he had been outsmarted in a trade.

So, by luck or the working of Providence, the two wanderers entered into the bounty of Eben Williams and his wife.

For the second time in as many years Ezra found that humanity is not the product of station or wealth. The Quakers worked with their hands, owned no slaves, had no heritage of power, yet they and the aristocratic Hamptons shared the same ideals of respect for man and belief in God. The Hampton sheets were of better quality than those he found in the Williams' house, but no cleaner or more refreshing to his aching body. The unknown farmer and the famous general had the same compassion for an injured boy, and their touch was equally gentle when they dressed his wounds. It was a privilege to learn such truths by experience.

The Quakers kept Ezra in bed for a week. He felt able to be up, but they said he must build a reserve of strength so they stuffed him as they might a Christmas turkey. Not until then did he realize how poor army fare had been. As he lay back after a meal of roast beef, vegetables, mince pie, cheese, and dainties he could not name, and thought of corn bread and bacon swimming in grease, he closed his eyes and shuddered.

"You know," he said to Mrs. Williams, "if the army spent more money on pie and less on gunpowder the war would be won sooner."

"Perhaps," she said, and her black eyes danced as they always did when she was amused, "if there had been more pie there would have been no war."

"Right!" Ezra slapped the blanket that covered him. "If all the politicians had been kept full of pie for the past few years they would have been too happy to think of fighting. That is, if it was the kind of pie you make."

"Thee flatters me." She flushed.

"I'm telling you the truth, ma'am. You should see the army cooks—or what we call cooks."

"Are they not trained for their work?"

"Trained? No, ma'am. We eat in messes of four or eight men and take turns cooking. Meal, flour, meat, grease thrown together any old way and called food. Not too much of it either."

"I would expect thee to be sick."

"We are sick. Half of us are always sick."

"Yet thee will return to the army?"

"Yes."

"Because it is thy duty?"

"I can't go back on my friends who are in it."

"And after the war?"

"I plan to go west with my uncle and build railroads." What a thrill it gave him to say that!

"May God spare thee and others like thee for thy work," she said. "The world needs its young men."

They never discussed the war at length. It was so pleasant to be away from it for a while that Ezra and Fess avoided mentioning it, though both knew that these peaceful days were only an interlude. For two more weeks they enjoyed themselves and Ezra grew so strong he was able to help Fess and the Quaker with some of the farm work. He found long hours to think about his Uncle George and the more he thought the more it seemed like a dream. In a way it was a dream, a hope, that gave new meaning to life and more substance to the menace of death by which they were surrounded.

One afternoon toward the last of June they heard the familiar sound of cannon fire in the far distance.

"Thunder?" Fess leaned on his pitchfork and looked blandly at the sky.

"You know it's not thunder," Ezra said.

They worked for a while in silence—the Quaker had gone to the mill with a grist—and then Fess remarked, "Wonder who's at it this time?"

"We should be there, Fess."

"Prob'ly Lee 'n' McClellan."

"I say we should be there," Ezra repeated.

"Bet you ol' Stonewall 'n' Gen'ral Hampton're in there."

"Did you hear what I said?" Ezra stepped in front of him.

"Shore, but that's a good twenty-five miles off. You hain't fitten to walk that far 'n' tote a gun."

"We can drive the mules."

"I promised 'em to Mr. Williams."

"Don't you aim ever to go back, Fess?"

"Pretty likely I do. But right now by the time we got there we wouldn't be no help 'cause you'd be tuckered out 'n' I'd have to take care of you. Give you another week here 'n' we'll both be in line."

"But those guns!" Ezra said tensely. "The general is there and Wade and Preston—while we are shirking."

"Bub," Fess said firmly, "you won't help none goin' back 'fore you can haul your share of the load. This war is a long ways from over. There'll be plenty of time for all of us to do our bit of fightin'. Go back 'fore you git your strength 'n' you'll be crossed off the roll for keeps. That's my say, now settle your own hash."

A feeling that Fess was probably right, plus a dread of being hospitalized again, kept Ezra at his work for six days. Occasionally, when the wind was right, the voice of the guns came over the horizon; then he breathed fast and his scalp prickled with excitement. It must be a mighty battle to last so long. He pictured it as a great storm drawing men into its center, hurling them against each other and leaving them broken.

The seventh morning, while he was dressing, Ezra heard a clattering of hoofs on the road and looked out the chamber window as six Union cavalrymen turned into the yard. Mr. Williams was leading a calf from the barn to a pasture and the horsemen surrounded him in a close circle.

"Say, Johnny, that critter's what we're looking for," one of them shouted as though he were half a mile away.

"The animal is not for sale," the Quaker answered.

"For sale!" The Yankee gave a short, barking laugh. "We don't buy from you rebels, we take."

"I have no part in war," Williams said quietly.

"I reckon not. Leggo that critter and make tracks."

"Not for thee," Williams said evenly, "not for thieves."

"I'll be damned!" the Yankee roared. "A lousy Quaker talking that way to us!"

"Called us thieves," another shouted, "called us Northerners thieves. We'll make him smart."

"Best thing to do," a Southern voice put in, "is to burn his barn 'n' roast the calf on the coals."

Behind the window curtain Ezra stopped throwing on his clothes and stood rigid. The blue-coated "Yankee" was Bert Sears. Ezra snatched his rifle from a corner and ran for the stairs.

"Fess," he shouted as he passed a door, "get your gun and turn out."

Before he reached the kitchen he heard a rifle crack upstairs. A wild yell rose outside, followed by a fusillade of shots. A bullet smashed the kitchen window and knocked a spoon out of Mrs. Williams' hand.

"Go down cellar," Ezra shouted to her. "There may be a fight."

"What does thee call this?" she asked placidly.

As he ran to the woodshed hoping to draw the fire away from her, he heard another shot upstairs. Outside a man screamed. Some one shouted, "There's soldiers here! Cut for it, boys!" Hoofs pounded. Ezra leaped into the yard and saw four of the Yankees riding down the road for dear life. He sent a shot after them, reloaded, and looked around for the other two. They lay in the driveway dead; the Quaker, still holding the calf, was staring at them.

Ezra walked over and looked at them, each shot neatly through the head.

"Fess is a good shot," he remarked to Williams.

"He killed them!" the Quaker gasped.

"Sure. I figure some of them pulled on you first."

"One drew a revolver, but I can't believe he would have harmed me."

"Those skunks would have plugged you like a rabbit."

"But Northerners are not savages."

"There are outlaws on both sides. By the way, I know one who got away. He's a Southerner. Hey, Fess," he shouted, as Fess came leisurely out of the house buttoning his shirt, "one of those birds was Bert Sears."

" 'Tain't surprisin'." Fess glanced sideways at the dead men as he walked over and caught the reins of the two cavalry horses that stood passively together. "Guess we sort of inherit these hosses—spoils of war. Good hosses, too, worth a hunderd 'n' thirty apiece."

Behind each saddle was a cloth sack partly filled with something that clinked when the horses moved. Ezra untied one and emptied it on the grass—a good two quarts of watches, finger rings, money and miscellaneous trinkets.

"They are robbers!" the Quaker cried.

"Worse than that," Ezra said. "They robbed the dead and wounded."

"Nice fellers," Fess commented.

"Man!" Ezra clicked his teeth angrily. "Why couldn't I have got some of them, too!"

"Guess you're in fightin' trim agin." Fess grinned. "Reckon we'll be headin' back for the war now."

"Reckon we will," Ezra agreed heartily.

Chapter 12

THE Seven Days' Battle was over before they reached the vicinity of it that afternoon. They were riding through thick woods that showed no signs of a struggle when they came into a clearing that held the ashes of farm buildings.

"Battle or varmints?" Ezra wondered aloud.

"Battle," Fess said. "Busted wagon 'n' dead hosses." He rose in his stirrups. "One hoss hain't dead. Put him outen his mis'ry, bub."

"Do it yourself, you saw him first."

"Don't like to shoot hosses, but it's worse to see 'em suffer." Fess rode over and looked down at a big black mare, struggling pitifully to get two broken legs under her. "Pore ol' lady, you didn't want no part in this war but you was drug into it. Git her 'tention, bub, so she won't see what I'm up to."

Ezra rode in front of the mare and waved his hat and as her eyes followed the motion Fess put a pistol bullet behind her ear.

"Hi, Johnnies!" a squeaky voice sang out back of them.

They spun around and faced a blue-coated soldier coming out of the woods.

"What you want, Yank?" Ezra asked, scanning the trees for an ambush.

"I ain't no Yank." The boy laughed. "Got these clo'es from

little Mac, the hero of Virginny. First hull pair of britches I've had in a year. An' lookit these shoes—bran' new!"

"What about the battle?" Ezra demanded.

"Say, where you been lately?"

"In a hospital. How did the battle come out?"

"We licked the hide off 'em. They dropped ever'thing 'n' run like rabbits. You oughter seen 'em go! 'N' you oughter see the stuff they left behind! Food! Mister man, jest heaps of it ever'wheres. Fancy stuff too—pickles, cheese, candy! We set right down 'n' et like hawgs."

"Comes natchel to some folks," Fess remarked pointedly.

"If you'd et only sticky flapjacks 'n' lard fer two months past you'd be hungry, Mister."

"Not hungry 'nough to steal from poor blue-bellies. Nossir, not me!" Fess wagged his head piously.

"You're jest pullin' my laig." The boy grinned.

"Never mind about him," Ezra cut in. "What about the army? Where is Hampton's Legion?"

"Dunno." The boy shrugged. "The army is all over ever'-wheres. There's a hull mess of it yonder." He jerked a thumb over his shoulder.

"Meanin' by that, any place 'twixt that rail fence 'n' the Atlantic Ocean," Fess remarked.

"Oh, come along, Fess, we've wasted enough time now." Ezra rode away.

As Fess followed he called out to the boy, "You're a nice little fellow. Look me up some time 'n' I'll make you a colonel. My name's Robert E. Lee."

"You're a big liar!" the boy shouted.

"I've a mind to sick my dog on you," Fess chuckled.

A mile beyond the woods they came to a highway where the backwash of battle was flowing. Lines of ambulances, loaded and empty, moved in opposite directions, the drivers hunched on the seats chewing tobacco as nonchalantly as though hauling firewood. Some of the lesser wounded plodded toward the rear or sat by the roadside resting and hoping for a ride. There was a new item of traffic this time, a string of freight wagons dragging captured horse feed back to a depot.

Fess commandeered a bag of oats and he and Ezra pulled into a field to feed their horses. They were sprawling on the grass, discussing their next move, when someone called from the barway, "Hello, troopers! Can you spare a bite for my horse?"

"Judas priest!" Fess rolled over and came up on his feet.

"Preston Hampton!" Ezra was up waving his hands.

"I'll be hanged!" Preston raised his slouch hat with a flourish. "It's you!"

"Bull's-eye," Fess agreed. "Git down 'n' I'll fodder the nag."

"I'll do it myself." Preston swung to the ground, slipped off the bridle, and dumped the oat bag in front of his horse. "We heard you were wounded, Ezra," he said over his shoulder.

"We both were and—"

"How is your father?" Fess interrupted.

"Fit as a fiddle. He escaped from home ten days ago."

"Escaped?"

"Yes." Preston laughed as he turned around. "They lionized him—parties, speeches, beautiful ladies swooning at his feet. He was more afraid than he ever was in battle, so he came back to the quiet and safety of the front just in time to help Lee wallop McClellan."

"I hear you tanned Little Mac's hide," Fess said.

"He is in full retreat." Preston looked at their horses. "So you picked up some of the booty, eh?"

"Abe Lincoln sent us these hosses," Fess explained.

Preston smiled. "Abe sent us mountains of supplies, but"— the smile was gone—"we paid the freight."

"Was it a tough battle?" Ezra asked.

"Yes. We may have lost twenty thousand all told."

"And the Yanks?"

"I don't know how many. They can afford it better than we can."

"You don't sound so perky," Fess observed. "What's wrong with winnin' a fight?"

"Nothing, Fess, not a thing. It's only that I am dog-tired. We had seven days and nights of it and now we are off again."

"Off where?"

"We have been assigned to help General Hill chase McClellan."

"Sounds like real pleasant work."

"Will we get our old places back in the legion?" Ezra asked.

"I suppose so." Preston stretched out on the grass. "Call me when my horse has eaten."

They rejoined Hampton's command that evening. Preston took them straight to his father's tent, for in that family personal friendships were of great importance. It was, in fact, a sort of family reunion, for the general's younger brother Frank, a lieutenant colonel, was there, a big, handsome man who loved mixing gaiety with soldiering, and young Wade was also present. Fess had been one of them since Cashier's Valley days and somehow Ezra was made to feel that he was not an outsider.

He was mostly silent, as became a youngster in such company, but his eyes and ears were open. Outwardly the general looked as usual, his face ruddy where not covered with beard, his gigantic body as straight and vigorous as ever. But there was a sadness in his eyes that had not been there before. Ezra did not know then that it came from the long, bitter hours he spent sorrowing for the men he had been obliged to sacrifice. And, too, for the enemies he had destroyed, for to him the misery of war was equally spread over both sides.

One thing was plain to Ezra. The general had come back from home dressed in odds and ends of clothing that had no resemblance to a uniform. His coat was plain gray and obviously prewar for it was civilian in cut with the collar turned down. The trousers were equally unmilitary. The cavalry boots were evidently the ones he had worn bear hunting. His hat was common brown felt with no pin or feather such as so many officers sported. No epaulets, no braid, just plain old clothes. Things were bad when the rank and file had to depend on the Yankees for their clothes, but they were worse when Wade Hampton could not replace a worn-out uniform.

When Ezra learned that Hampton's cavalry was to lead the pursuit of McClellan he pictured a wild pell-mell chase, with the bluecoats pulling out straight and the whole thing ending in a few hours. But that was not the way it worked out. McClellan had lost the Peninsula Campaign and was leaving Virginia, but it was an orderly retreat and his army of a hundred thousand was many times larger than the pursuing force. The Confederate plan was to follow close, keep the enemy on the move and give him no time to save his immense stores. It was carried out nicely, though so slowly that not until the first of September did Hampton feel it had been completed. Then he was allowed no rest because Lee, Jackson and Longstreet had been drubbing another Union army, commanded by General Pope, at Second Manassas and the legion troopers were ordered to come hotfoot and join the pursuit.

In the meantime General Lee had finished reorganizing the Army of Northern Virginia. There were now two corps of infantry under Jackson and Longstreet respectively, and also a division of cavalry. This was commanded by Major General J. E. B. Stuart, a dashing, rollicking youngster of twenty-nine who was perhaps the best cavalry officer ever seen in America. Some said Wade Hampton was as good or better. Lee's opinion of Hampton was so high that he asked him to be second-in-command, as Stuart's senior brigadier. There was strenuous work ahead for the cavalry and it was feared that Hampton, who was forty-four years old, might not be equal to full leadership. He had more initiative and endurance than any of his troopers, but by army standards he was old and therefore must have lost his edge. This was a joke among his men, especially with Festival Jones who was well past forty himself.

During the next three months, while they chased Pope and fought McClellan again, this time in Maryland, Ezra grew to admire the gay young officers in Stuart's division. In battle they fought like devils and loved it; on the march they took more than their share of hardship without grumbling; in camp they sang and danced and joked and drank Yankee liquor for the pure joy of living.

There was Jeb Stuart himself, not large of stature but hard as flint, with fierce red whiskers almost hiding a long, merry face. How that man could roar orders on the field and then, when the campfires were twinkling, how sweetly he could sing as he tickled a banjo! He was a great dresser, plumed hat, red-lined cape, elbow-length gauntlets and all, but he was no sissy, being crafty as a fox and brave almost to the point of foolhardiness. And there were the plump but active Fitzhugh Lee and tall Rooney Lee, nephew and son respectively of the commander, huge von Borcke, the Prussian dragoon, Captain Cooke who had been a successful poet before the war, and many others whose talents, grim and gay, blended in the one purpose of giving their beloved cause everything they had.

On September twenty-two the army that had been marching and fighting almost continuously since spring camped at Martinsburg, Virginia. They were weary beyond words, and those who had eaten all their Federal rations were hungry again. Most of the gray uniforms had been replaced by Union blue or the yellow-brown "butternut" shade of the dye made from copperas and walnut hulls. They had lost more than thirty-five thousand men, yet their morale was good; the Yankees had lost twice as many and been beaten at every turn.

For a week the men relaxed and tried to catch up on things they had neglected during the campaign. They slept, wrote letters, mended clothing, deloused themselves with hot water and smudges, and wandered around gossiping and reeling off tall stories. Jeb Stuart and his cronies went to dances given in their honor by nearby planters, where the general and Fitzhugh Lee behaved as gallantly as knights from the pages of a book. General Hampton, in his old clothes, sought out the hunters and fishermen of the neighborhood and, while swapping adventure yarns with them, learned the lay of the land and the secrets of the surrounding country.

Most of this carefree gaiety was a blind to foil the many spies who hung about the camp. The Confederate leaders had no wish either to take things easy themselves or to allow the enemy to do so. They went about quietly questioning their subordinates, talking with individual troopers, and examining horses and equipment. Something was in the wind. On October ninth six hundred men in each of the three brigades got orders to report at nearby Darksville. Every one of the eighteen hundred was known for his ability to ride, shoot and think for himself, and every horse was in top condition. When Ezra found that he was included in the elite troop he felt a thrill second only to the time he joined the legion.

As he and Fess rode into the Darksville camp Rooney Lee was calling some of the men together.

"Boys," he shouted, holding up a paper, "this is an order from General Stuart. Listen, and remember what it says.

"*Soldiers: You are about to engage in an enterprise which, to insure success, imperatively demands at your hands coolness, decision and bravery; implicit obedience to orders without question or cavil, and the strictest order of sobriety on the march and in bivouac. The destination and extent of this expedition had better be kept to myself than known to you. Suffice it to say that, with the hearty cooperation of officers and men, I have not a doubt of its success—a success which will reflect credit in the highest degree upon your arms. The orders which are herewith published for your government are absolutely necessary and must be strictly enforced.*"

"Looks like we're goin' on a coon hunt," Fess piped up. "I've a notion Jeb thinks the best coon pelts grow north of the Potomac."

Young Wade Hampton heard the remark and laughed his big laugh.

"Be I right?" Fess cocked an eye at him.

"For all I know, you aren't," Wade told him. "But it is possible your dog Spot may have to swim."

That evening General Stuart put a fresh plume in his hat and rode away to a party. When it was dark Hampton ordered the troopers to mount quietly, then, leaving the fires burning, led them down the road toward McCoy's Ford. Ezra breathed hard as he took his place in the long, dim line of horsemen. This was what he had dreamed of, following Wade Hampton blindly into the night on a mysterious mission. The silent stealth of it appealed to his sense of adventure more than a headlong charge in daylight, and he wanted to sing to the music of creaking saddles and the flowing stream of hoof-beats. Here, at last, was the glamour of war and, because he knew it was of passing duration, he made the most of it.

They kept on at a walk, with the cool autumn wind in their faces, no one speaking, everyone wondering. Up a hill and then, not far away, they saw the twinkle of stars in the Potomac. Into the water without pause, stirrups high, hundreds of feet splashing, hundreds of iron shoes clicking in muffled tones against the stones in the river bed, up the other bank and past two watching officers outlined against the sky—the gigantic Hampton and the smaller, square-built Stuart, whose devil-may-care stance showed even in the gloom.

It was Maryland soil under their feet now and words were not necessary to tell them they were going north on a raid. There were enemy pickets not far from the river, but they were playing cards and were snapped up like roosting chickens. Dawn broke soon after that and fog flowed into the valley so that no one saw them as they trotted six miles north to Hagerstown Pike. This highway was a Federal supply line and was equipped with signal stations. Some leaders might have tried slipping by it in the mist and postponing discovery as long as possible, but Jeb Stuart was not that kind. He wanted to needle the Yankees as early and often as he could, so he destroyed the first station and went on, laughing at what the enemy would say when their messages failed to go through.

About noon they crossed the Pennsylvania line and the raid was on in earnest. There had been no rough stuff in Maryland, which was friendly to the South, but Ezra supposed when they entered enemy territory they would cut loose. These people were Yanks, so why shouldn't their property become the spoils of war? But Stuart and Hampton were not of that mind. To them pillaging, even in a small way, was plain stealing and it was not to be said that the Confederate Army was a gang of thieves. Singing was allowed—Stuart often led it—but there was no wild yelling and whooping unbecoming to gentlemen. When they entered a town they took what they needed from the stores in the way of food and clothing and in payment gave receipts so the claims might be brought against the United States Government. Horses were acquired in the same way. Officers usually paid cash for their coffee and tobacco. No soldier was allowed to enter a building except on business and the rights of citizens were rigidly respected. The only destruction was to property that might be useful to the Federal Army, such as supply depots, railroads, bridges and telegraph lines.

In that way they went through Mercersburg and Chambersburg, camping outside the latter place for the night. They knew well enough that soldiers, militia and civilians would be swarming upon them from all directions like bees whose hive had been disturbed, but they ate a rousing supper and slept well. Ezra carried a final message from Hampton to one of the outpost captains, then turned in and fell asleep to the sound of a banjo and plantation songs in Stuart's tent.

After breakfast Stuart cantered across the town square to where Hampton sat on his big brown horse watching the troopers fall into line.

"Ready, General?" He raised his plumed hat.

"Ready, sir."

"Then," Stuart shouted for the benefit of nearby civilians, "we are off to Gettysburg twenty miles to the east."

"Where did he say we are going?" Preston leaned toward Ezra.

"Sounded like Gettysburg."

"Never heard of the place before and probably won't again. If I know Jeb Stuart, we will head in the opposite direction."

They did, swinging south along the Hagerstown Pike, scouring the country for more horses, cutting telegraph lines, chasing an occasional Federal scout and having a great time. Toward evening they trotted back into Maryland, dusty, tired and happy. At Emmitsburg they were greeted as heroes, given a free lunch, and asked to stay for a ball. Stuart wanted to accept, but his scouts dragged in a Federal messenger with dispatches revealing that a force of Union horse and foot was racing to cut off his retreat. He said a few pleasant words to his hosts and galloped away after his men. They were already pushing hard toward Poolesville, where they would cross the Potomac into Virginia.

Hampton led the march that night, being famous for his ability to find his way in unfamiliar country. They rode as fast as their weary horses could go and clattered through Middleburg at eleven o'clock.

"Fess," Hampton said, when they were beyond the town, "I want you and Ezra to change to fresh horses and fall out

here. If the pursuit comes up before daylight learn their number and overtake us."

"That's what we'll do, Gen'ral," Fess accepted cheerfully.
"Come along, bub, let's see how well we can swap hosses in
the dark."

They switched their saddles to a couple of led mounts and
sat down in a field beside the road, the reins in their fingers.

"You take a nap, I'll watch," Fess offered.

"No, you first."

"Can't for a while. I've got to pick the burrs offen Spot. He
got plastered chasin' a rabbit this afternoon."

"You're a queer duck, Fess."

"Hain't I though! What's more, I enjoy it. Go to sleep."

It seemed to Ezra he had slept only a moment before Fess
touched his foot.

"Sounds like Abe's boys're out ridin'," he said leisurely.

Ezra got up and, after a moment, made out the distant
sounds of a body of moving horsemen.

"Hold our hosses by the nose so's they can't whinney,"
Fess ordered, as they moved behind some bushes.

There was no moon but the stars were bright enough to
show the road. The clicking of horseshoes against stones, the
clattering of scabbards and the creaking of saddles approached. A man rode by alone, then a double line of horsemen. Ezra began counting the heads as they passed, outlined
against the sky. Troop after troop passed at a walk, obviously
dog-tired. Then came half a dozen pieces of light artillery and
their caissons, and finally, after an interval, two riders.

"This blasted girth is slipping again," one growled.

They stopped opposite the bushes while one jumped to the ground and worked at his saddle.

"How far is it to that place called Frederick?" the other asked.

"I don't know, but I heard old Pleasonton say we will get there before morning and cut off the Johnnies." He mounted.

"We'd better. McClellan will give us hell if so much as one of Stuart's men gets away." They rode on.

Ezra and Fess followed them. Clouds were blowing up in the west and in a few minutes the sky was dark.

"You do the talkin'," Fess whispered. "You sound more like a Yank."

They broke into a gallop and overtook the other two, who challenged them.

"Couriers from headquarters," Ezra snapped.

"The old man is up front."

"Thanks."

Ezra pulled out on the left and, followed by Fess, passed the long column at a sharp trot. The leader heard them coming and dimly they saw him swing his horse around.

"Who are you?" he demanded in a big voice.

"Jefferson Davis and party," Ezra answered gaily as they dug in their spurs.

Pistol shots cracked behind them, an order was shouted, a bugle sounded and the whole troop thundered down the pike. But their horses were tired and the night was dark; it was no use and they soon gave it up. An hour or so later the scouts overtook the raiders and reported to Hampton that eight hundred cavalry and six pieces of artillery under Pleasonton planned to intercept him in Frederick before daybreak.

"Fine work, boys, fine work!" the general said heartily.

"By Jove!" Stuart spoke up in the darkness. "That should earn commissions for both of you."

"Thanks all the same, Gen'ral," Fess answered quietly, "but I hired out to help my neighbor, Gen'ral Hampton. That keeps me so busy I hain't got time to be an officer."

"The same with me, thank you, sir," Ezra added.

"My word!" Stuart's voice vibrated. "Hampton, it is you who deserve promotion, for inspiring such loyalty in your men."

"Neighborly ties are strong in the Carolinas," Hampton said softly. Then in his usual tone, "I suggest, Stuart, that we avoid Frederick and take a shorter route to White's Ford."

"Lead the way, sir," Stuart said. "Your nose is better than mine in the dark."

In the cold, wet dawn they waded the Potomac and from the Virginia shore waved mockingly to Pleasonton, who had arrived too late to annoy their crossing. Without losing a man they had ridden back and forth through the enemy lines, destroying supplies and communications and picking up twelve hundred horses. It was a job well down, a brilliant piece of work, and Jeb Stuart rode home with new ideas bubbling in his active brain. Thoughtfully Wade Hampton watched him and hoped the ebullient youngster would be able to keep his feet on the ground.

Chapter 13

THE success of the raid was more than material; it demonstrated that a well-handled force of cavalry could ride almost at will through and behind the Union lines, doing heavy damage and returning safely with booty. If it could be done once, why not again on a larger scale? Possibly it was the seed from which grew Lee's plan of Northern invasion. It left McClellan's face red and swamped him with such a deluge of criticism that command of the Army of the Potomac was soon given to General Ambrose Burnside.

There were times when it seemed strange to Ezra that he, like practically all the men and a majority of the officers, knew little of what was happening on other fronts. From young Wade and Preston he heard considerable about the war along the Mississippi, largely because the Yankees were ravaging some plantations their father owned in that section. The Shenandoah Valley, where Stonewall Jackson was doing unkind things to another Union army, was near enough to be almost of local interest. But from other points war news was vague and unsatisfactory. Newspapers were scarce because of paper and ink shortages and such letters as reached the troops were weeks late and usually personal in nature. To Ezra, who had never formed the newspaper habit or received a letter in his life, such things did not matter much. He was too busy to be bored or to have long thoughts about other people's battles.

All the while, as time permitted, he was trying to learn what had become of his uncle. Finally in September General Hampton, in whom he had confided, located the captain in a prison camp. He wrote him a letter promising to arrange for his exchange as soon as possible. Ezra also sent him a letter, an epistle of great labor, for he was by no means sure of himself on paper. Both were courteously acknowledged by Marsh, who expressed his appreciation and hoped to thank them personally at the close of "this unhappy incident called war," as he put it. Despite being wounded and imprisoned, it was still an incident to him. Then, less than a month later, they learned he had escaped.

"Why didn't the man wait for his exchange?" Hampton said critically. "Why take an unnecessary risk?"

"I believe, sir," Ezra said, "he wants to be free to fight again, not tied up by his parole."

"He enjoys fighting, eh?"

"No, sir, but he wants to do what he can to end the war and go on to building railroads."

"Take my advice, Ezra, if your uncle is that zealous to do constructive work, follow him. This broken country needs millions like him."

For a time both armies sat on the banks of the Potomac and looked at each other without exchanging shots. Then Burnside moved across the river with a hundred thousand men and Lee, who had little more than half as many, pulled back south of the Rappahannock. The Union commander might well have pressed for a battle, but it was November, the weather was turning cold and he decided to settle down for the winter.

Almost overnight the Confederate army laid aside its guns and took up its axes. There had never been many tents and now those were badly worn, so the men pitched in to build log huts. Hampton, with a woodsman's instinct, chose a camp site in the heaviest timber available, where there was good drainage and plenty of water. Some officers tried to organize their building program in an orderly fashion, but every man more or less worked out his own plan. The result was a village of dwellings ranging from dugouts up through half cabins with canvas roofs, huts with stick-and-mud walls and log mansions with several rooms. The heating arrangements were equally varied. Some had fire pits below the floor level with smoke holes in the roof, in others perforated kettles hung from the rafters, a few had stoves, but the majority depended on stone-and-mud fireplaces. These habitations were furnished with anything their owners could build, steal or win in card games: bunks, benches, tables, stools, boxes, flour-barrel chairs and even writing desks and bookcases. On the walls hung such utensils as the mess happened to have, from teaspoons to washtubs.

Such cabins accommodated from two to eight men. Fess, Ezra and two other country-bred troopers teamed up and built a snug one about fifteen feet square, using their horses and picket ropes to haul the logs and thereby winning a quart of Yankee whisky offered by their colonel for the first house completed. Soon one of the men died of pneumonia and the other got a furlough from which he never returned. Fess took one of the empty bunks for Spot and suggested that Ezra find himself a similar pet now they had room for it.

"Honest to Moses," Ezra said, "sometimes I think you are the queerest man on earth."

"Hain't I though!" Fess agreed heartily. "My pa used to say iffen he owed a travelin' circus a carload of freaks 'n' it wouldn't take me in full payment he'd beat 'em out of the debt."

"And that was before you owned an imaginary dog, too."

"Yeh. You know, bub, there's a lot to be said for such a dog. One thing, he don't eat a lot of rations."

"Who does eat a lot of rations in this army?"

"Well, we've still got some Yankee grub left."

"A little. We're better off than the infantry."

"Serves 'em right for bein' infantry. Walkin' soldiers!"

"But they get hungry just the same. Have you heard rations have been cut again?"

"Cut where? Both ends 'n' the middle has been gone for weeks."

"Cut to eighteen ounces of flour and four ounces of bacon a day."

"That won't be so bad iffen we git half of it, which we won't. Pretty soon they'll tell us to lay on our backs 'n' lap moonlight for supper."

"And clothes!" Ezra made a hopeless gesture. "If it wasn't for Yank uniforms three-quarters of us would be naked. As it is, we look like beggars."

"There's some advantage in that," Fess pointed out cheerfully, picking up a shirt and examining it for lice. "You can tell a man's rank from behind—one hole in the seat of his britches means he's a captain, two holes is a lieutenant, no seat at all is a private."

"You're lucky to see the funny side of it," Ezra said gloomily. "I'm beginning to wonder who will win this war."

Fess spun around and threw the shirt in his face. "Iffen we all talked that way there'd be no question as to who'll win."

"Oh, cool off. I'm as good a soldier as you are."

"Then shut up that talk."

"I'll shut up when I get good and ready. If you don't like it, get out. And take your dog with you."

At that critical moment a knock sounded on the door and Preston stuck his head inside.

"We are going on a coon hunt." He bayed like a hound. "Report in an hour."

"Company headquarters?" Fess asked.

"No, brigade. Father is taking only a few men." He was gone, whistling a tune that faded into the twilight.

Neither spoke as they ate supper—Yankee crackers and salt beef washed down with Rappahannock water. It seemed silly to be by the ears for no good reason, but neither would give in. Fess laid a bone by the fire for Spot and followed Ezra down to the pine woods that served as a stable. Each was given four quarts of oats, precious fodder that was kept for special purposes, and while the horses ate, the men went over their equipment.

The wind of late November was cold and the stars looked

shrunken and unfriendly in their remoteness. Young Wade and Preston rode up carrying bull's-eye lanterns which they hung on the branch of a pine, facing in opposite directions. Their father appeared and stopped in the light, looking pleased, for this was his raid. A bugle might be heard by Union pickets, so he called to the men he had chosen and they came from all sides, a hundred and fifty of them. He motioned them to form columns and led them quietly out of the woods and across the river.

Ezra rode beside a Georgian who hiccoughed and swore under his breath because he could not stop.

"Too much red-eye," Ezra jibed softly.

"Too much—hic—grease. Fat pork makes me—hic—gag. What wouldn't Ah give fer some—hic—ripe peaches!"

Ezra didn't know where Fess was, nor did he care. The clatter of hoofs on the road made him want to sing as he leaned forward in his saddle, feeling himself part of a great force. A mighty force when you remembered the whole Confederate Army and the eight million people behind it! Of course they would win. He had been a fool to suggest they might not. And Fess had been a fool to get sore about it. That was Fess, calm as an oyster in a pinch but flying off the handle at some little thing. Queer duck.

They trotted on through country that was familiar even at night, for they had often ridden there before the retreat from the Potomac. When they stopped on a hill and saw campfires in the distance they knew it was a small encampment at the crossroads of Harwood Church. Hampton planned the surprise as carefully as he would a major engagement, for in his opinion what was worth doing was worth doing the best way. He sent detachments to close in from three sides, calculated the distance they would travel and the time they would need, and then led the rest of his troopers down the main road at a walk. Not until he was challenged by a picket did he raise an alarm, but then his big voice roared out, his men answered with a yell and they charged.

The enemy was a small company of Union cavalry, about a hundred, most of them asleep around fires made from a nearby rail fence. They jumped up, trailing blankets, grabbing weapons, bumping into each other, all too confused to put up an orderly fight—or any kind of stand. They were surrounded before they awoke and when they got to their feet each one thought he was covered by at least six Johnny Rebs.

"We are your prisoners," their colonel shouted, running around in his stocking feet. He added with a rueful grin, "I can't offer my sword because I can't find it."

"Never mind." Hampton smiled. "I suggest that you search for your boots first."

The haul yielded ninety-two men and one hundred horses. No one was wounded on either side. It was a small engagement but perfectly executed. The horses were so badly needed for replacements that Hampton decided not to risk losing them by extending the raid, so he turned back to his camp in Stevensburg, across the Rappahannock.

As they trotted through the darkness Ezra found himself riding beside a prisoner.

"Been in the army long, Yank?" he asked.

"Two years."

"Like it?"

"Up to now."

"You won't have to fight any more."

"You won't have much more of it either, Johnny. The South gets its coup de grâce any time now."

"It's what?"

"French for knockout."

"You must be educated. Ever read *Ivanhoe*?"

"Yes."

"It's a wonderful book, eh?"

"You Southerners would like it. We are not so romantic in the North."

"Don't get huffy, Yank," Ezra said pleasantly. "One more question—I ask it of every Yank I meet—do you know a feller named Bert Sears?"

"No."

"Thank you."

It was dawn when Ezra returned to the cabin. Fess sat by the fire smoking a cigar he had taken from a prisoner.

"Mornin', bub." He spoke as though nothing had happened, and Ezra decided to let it go that way. "Nice little raid."

"Yes." Ezra held his red hands to the blaze. "I hope we have more of them."

"Looks like we will. I been talkin' with Preston. He says raids're gittin' pop'lar at headquarters—Hampton, Stuart, Lee —ever'body goin' for 'em. Lee himself might try one some time, take the hull army north."

"Let's eat breakfast first." Ezra smiled wearily. "What'll you have, crackers and salt beef or salt beef and crackers?"

These small raids were profitable to the Confederates as well as annoying to the enemy. Two weeks later Hampton took five hundred men and hit the Union supply depot at Dumfries, picking up more than fifty prisoners and a whole string of loaded wagons. Then his men spread out, cut telegraph wires, ripped up railroads and created such alarm that an entire Federal corps was sent to chase them home. Again not a man was wounded. It was fun breaking loose that way, though the last time three days and nights in the snow meant real hardship for the Southerners. When they returned to camp they were chagrined and elated to learn that during their absence Burnside had suddenly come to life only to be well thrashed at Fredericksburg by an army half his size. The promised coup de grâce was not doing well.

Despite the victory, the Confederate camp was a gloomy place. Many of the huts were vacated forever by their builders, and the cold, dreary field hospitals were full of wounded men. Ezra was shocked to see how shortages of medicine, bandages and blankets had increased since he was a patient. The soup he once loathed because it was thick and sticky had now been diluted to little more than water colored with corn meal. Strips of hard, clammy tent cloth had replaced worn-out blankets. The only warm drink a shivering man could get was sassafras tea. There was so little soap that everyone and everything had a dirty look.

Hampton gave the hospitals what food he could spare and then, a few days before Christmas, galloped again across the river, hitting at the Telegraph Road, which was a Federal artery of supply. Union cavalry was on guard there but he got away with a hundred and fifty prisoners and twenty wagonloads of sutlers' holiday goods. What celestial fare that was: hams, lemons, sugar, oranges, coffee, pickles, candy, brandy, wine and other unbelievable items! When his men brought him a keg of wine tagged for General Burnside he could not refuse it as a Christmas gift, though he rarely touched liquor.

Jeb Stuart had a gay Christmas party; then, with a new plume in his hat and an old song on his lips, he led eighteen hundred picked troopers to the favorite hunting ground of Telegraph Road. That was a wild ride, as all rides were when Stuart led. For nearly a week they galloped and shot and whooped through Federal territory. Sometimes they walked to warm their feet and again they dozed in their saddles, big Frank Hampton nearly falling off and being unmercifully teased about it. They routed two regiments of Union cavalry and seized a railway station, from where Stuart telegraphed Federal headquarters, complaining of the poor condition of the mules he had captured. They lost one man and a dozen were wounded, but the others reached camp safely on January 1, 1863, with two hundred prisoners and much booty.

So it went throughout the winter, raiding, resting, raiding again. The men with Stuart and Hampton were the envy of the infantry that led a monotonous life behind the lines and suffered from low morale. Ezra was happy, for he was having adventure with a minimum of the bloodshed he hated. It was a colorful life for the men, but so destructive to horses that in the early spring the brigade was sent into southern Virginia to recuperate mounts and get fresh ones. While there they heard the rousing news of victory at Chancellorsville, and in the next breath the details of Stonewall Jackson's tragic death there. The great, bearded leader, who possessed the religious fervor and military might of an Old Testament hero, had been accidentally shot down by his own men.

The brigade rejoined Stuart in May at Orange Court House. The weather was beautiful and invited to things more pleasant than war.

"Can't blame the boys for goin' off on furlough, or jest goin' off 'n' fergittin' to come back," Fess said one day as they polished their spurs and buckles.

"They're skulkers," Ezra said shortly.

"Mebbe so, mebbe not. There's corn to be planted 'n' families to be took care of."

"And a war to be fought, too. I read in a newspaper there are seventy-five thousand deserters this minute. Think what Lee could do if he had those men!"

"Yeh." Fess spat thoughtfully on his cloth, dipped it in sand and went on polishing. "Back in Cashier's Valley the birds're singin', 'n' the fish're bitin', like they did when Wade Hampton 'n' me was boys there. Me, I'm down here fightin' for states rights—or somethin'."

"States rights my eye! You're fighting for General Hampton. If he was on the North side you'd be there too."

" 'N' you, bub?" Fess smiled slyly.

"Sure. Political questions don't mean much to me because I don't understand 'em, but I understand my friends and I'll go with 'em to the end of the road. And I want to get this war over with and get to doing something constructive."

"That's a big word."

"There's a lot in it when you think it over as I've done lately."

"I s'pose so." Fess threw away his rag and straightened his back. "There! Now I'm all shined up to go call on Old Abe."

"Are you drunk?"

"Me?" Fess scratched one of his huge fuzzy ears. "I'm as sober as seven deacons settin' on a rail fence. Ever'body knows the army's fixin' to start north. It hain't fer to Washin'-ton."

"I don't think General Lee tells you his plans."

"That's all right, I don't tell him mine neither." Fess walked away with a shrug.

Whatever its commander's plans might be, it was soon obvious that the Army of Northern Virginia was preparing to move. Stuart's cavalry now numbered nearly ten thousand men, who were assembled at Culpepper on June five for a grand review. They called it Jeb's party for it reflected the young leader's gay spirit, with dancing, maneuvers, fiery speeches and a ball in the evening. Hampton looked in on the dance, where his brother and two sons were doing the family proud in social style. It was the last time they would laugh together that way.

Three days later the five brigades of horsemen, with the light artillery, camped at Brandy Station and as the roosters began to crow they fanned out toward the string of fords on the Rappahannock. By then every rider knew he was helping screen the advance of the infantry, which would follow later in three corps under Hill, Ewell and Longstreet.

However, the Federals had gotten wind of Stuart's activity and figured he was taking his whole force north on a gigantic raid. Furthermore, by this time the Yankees had plenty of cavalry and knew how to use it. During the night they had moved ten thousand men close to the river where, just at daylight, their artillery opened on the first of Stuart's men, and half the blue riders crossed the river to see what was there. They found the surprised Confederates widely separated, as each brigade had been assigned a different ford.

For several hours after that it seemed to Ezra that the two armies were playing tag. During most of the forenoon he carried messages from Hampton to other officers within a radius of four miles. Sometimes he found them where they were supposed to be, but usually somewhere else, which necessitated galloping back and forth asking questions and dodging Union regiments that seemed equally lost. It was called skirmishing and he knew each side was trying to get into position to drive home a blow.

Toward noon he met Fess, who was similarly busy, and they pulled up their dripping horses.

"Where the devil can I find Stuart?" Ezra demanded.

"Fleetwood Heights. Know where that is?" Fess wiped his dust-crusted face.

"Yes. It's the only place in Virginia I haven't been this morning." Ezra gathered up his reins.

"Hold on!" Fess put out a hand. "Now you tell me where Butler's Second South Caroliny is."

"On the Stevensburg Road."

"Much obliged, bub. We'll git this army together iffen we have to ketch 'em one to a time 'n' tie 'em." Fess trotted on his way.

Ezra found Stuart and delivered Hampton's note, which the general read and pocketed with a nod. On a rise of ground he sat his favorite little horse as jauntily as at a review.

"There will be no reply," he said. "Fortunately General Hampton will soon join us here."

Fortunately indeed. Ezra could see there had been fighting on the hill, at the foot of which the Union cavalry was now massing. To him it looked like a blue horde far exceeding the number of men behind Stuart. Any soldier could see that if they gained the heights they would dominate the field and be able to fight on their own terms.

They were coming, but even as they began to move long lines of Confederate horsemen poured out of the woods and flowed in waves toward the base of the hill. Ezra could see the big general leading on the left, while toward the center the teams of Hart's Battery ran belly to the ground. On th right was the Cobb Legion, the First South Carolina, First North Carolina and the Jeff Davis Legion. The sound o their hoofs was one great roll of thunder. Their sabers gleamed and their flags rode evenly in the wind.

The Federals wheeled to meet them. Hart's Battery swun around with magnificent precision, and almost before th traces slackened the guns began slamming case shot into the blue mass. A moment later Hampton's line crashed in. The Federals reeled back up the hill, horses rearing, riders slashing as they crouched low or stood in their stirrups. Above the tumult rose a mighty clatter as thousands of swords met in the air.

Two Confederate regiments circled and slashed the enemy's flanks. The blue line broke and galloped up the hill, where Stuart's horse and batteries were nearly run over. Artillerymen were swept from their pieces and fought back with swab sticks and rammers. They regained their guns and resumed firing so furiously that Hampton had to stop his men to avoid being mowed down by friends. Before the cannoneers saw what they were doing, the Federals escaped into the woods in the direction of Brandy Station.

For all he considered himself a seasoned trooper, Ezra completely lost his head during those furious minutes. Afterward he could recall none of the details, memory held nothing but a sweeping, bursting sense of exultation as he rode with Jeb Stuart, slashing and thrusting and yelling. This was no raid, it was a battle of knights fighting sword to sword as Ivanhoe fought. It was, in fact, the first great cavalry battle of the war. With a soldier's egotism, Ezra supposed he had taken part in the only action of consequence. Later in the day, when he rejoined Hampton and was helping chase the Yankees across the river, reports of other bloody clashes came in.

"General Hampton, sir?" A little lieutenant on a lathered horse pulled up and saluted.

"I am he." Hampton leaned out and took a note from the youngster's hand. He read it and leaned heavily on the saddle pommel.

"What is it, Father?" young Wade asked.

"Your uncle Frank has fallen."

"Dead?"

"Not yet."

That night Ezra and Fess waited outside a house near Stevensburg.

"Frank fit like a Hampton," Fess said softly. "We was outnumbered, but he didn't run. He was sword fightin' with a Yank when another of 'em shot him through the body. We picked him up 'n' lugged him in here." Fess kicked the ground. "Gawd, bub, he was a han'some man! 'N' a good man. 'N' a happy man."

"He may pull through, Fess."

"Been gone for minutes. I felt it."

The door opened, and General Hampton and his two sons came out.

"All over, Fess," the general said quietly.

"Yes, sir." Fess bowed his head.

Chapter 14

LARGELY because of what Stuart and Hampton did at Brandy Station, and their active presence farther east during the next two weeks, Lee was able to march his army along the Shenandoah Valley and across the Potomac without being detected. That the Union scouts were never able to get near enough to learn what was going on was high praise for the Confederate cavalry. The Northern invasion was on and Stuart was jubilant; Hampton was pleased though thoughtful, for he took a sober view of the campaign as a whole.

On the evening of June twenty-third, as Ezra sat outside brigade headquarters for a possible last message of the day, Stuart cantered up. Whistling a tune, he swung to the ground and hurried inside. It was characteristic of him to call on his officers rather than sending for them, as it kept him in motion.

"Good evening, Hampton!" His voice came through the canvas wall. "We have our orders."

"Indeed, General!"

"If Hooker doesn't cause trouble, I'll leave two brigades to keep an eye on things and join Lee with the others."

"You will do so at once, sir?" Hampton sounded relieved.

"No. General Lee leaves it to my judgment as to whether I can cut around the Federals, worrying them and picking up supplies, before joining him east of the mountains."

"That is a heavy responsibility, sir."

"Don't be so cautious, Hampton." Stuart laughed. "Of course we can do it. I shall leave Jones and Robertson behind. The rest of us muster at Salem tomorrow and strike out."

"May I ask if you will retain contact with the Army of Northern Virginia, sir?" Hampton inquired.

"With Ewell's Corps, perhaps." Stuart sounded impatient. "I know what you are thinking, Hampton, but don't worry. We shall move fast and join Lee before he needs us. Good night, General! Salem in the morning." He was out and away, picking up the tune where he had dropped it.

After a few minutes Hampton came to the tent door and asked, "Are you still on duty, Ezra?"

"Yes, sir."

"You are relieved for the night. Get your rest while you can." He closed the tent flap and Ezra heard him walking back and forth.

Four days later they were in Maryland where, near Rockville, they picked up an enemy train of a hundred and twenty-five wagons, teams and harness. They swept on to within four miles of Washington and courteously made prisoners of a picnic party because it contained some government officials. These were quickly paroled along with four hundred other Federals whose presence slowed up the raiders. As a boy might long to break up a rival's birthday party, Stuart ached to dash into the city. Oh, the fun of it and the glory of it! But even he dared not yield to the temptation. So he tore up some of the Baltimore and Ohio railroad, burned a few bridges, cut some telegraph wires, and turned north without serious opposition from the surprised Yankees. Stuart was in high spirits, but Hampton was worried because they had completely lost touch with Lee's army.

On the last day of June they entered Pennsylvania, strangely enough behind the Federal army that was finally going North to meet Lee. At Hanover they had a successful brush with Union troops and learned from newspapers there that Lee had been in York two days before.

"A heck of an idea!" Ezra grumbled. "We must depend on civilians to tell us where the blue-bellies are."

"Shut up!" Fess snapped. He was having one of his grumpy days. "When Jeff Davis wants you to run things, he'll tell you."

"Go feed your dog," Ezra retorted. "He wants some of that hot-air soup you're so good at making." Ezra rode away and left him.

It was obvious that the two great armies were approaching each other and would soon clash. Stuart was anxious now, but the best his scouts could do was to bring in vague reports that Lee was near Dover. Stuart headed in that direction and rode his command all night so hard that some of his weary men fell out of their saddles.

There was no sign of Lee when they reached the town in the morning. The troopers had to rest, but some of the young officers got fresh horses and continued the search. In the afternoon Stuart took the road to Carlisle, hoping at least to find food for his famished men and horses. They were so near complete exhaustion that when they saw the place was defended, though by only two hundred state militia, they lacked the energy to attack. They went into camp hungry and were depressed by the feeling that they had wasted their strength on a wild-goose chase.

The evening the officers returned with orders from General Lee himself. Ezra got the story from Preston as he helped him unsaddle. Preston was so tired he staggered.

"They are fighting at Gettysburg," he said. "Meade is the new Federal commander. He has ninety thousand men."

"Then we are outnumbered," Ezra said.

"It wouldn't be so bad if General Lee had been able to choose his ground. But he was forced to fight there because of—because he lacked information of Meade's whereabouts."

"Because we weren't there to scout for him."

"Oh, I didn't say that, Ezra!" Preston's drawn face twitched in the lantern light. "Nor did General Lee imply it. But"— he hesitated—"he does need Stuart and father badly and quickly."

A bugle call ripped through the darkness.

"Lord! We're starting now." Preston picked up his saddle and slapped it on his horse. "Look!" He caught Ezra by the arm. "Don't repeat what you just said, about not being there when we were needed. It might sound like criticism of our commander."

"Not a word. But," Ezra could not help adding, "you know as well as I do that it wouldn't have happened if General Stuart had listened to your father."

"Silence, Private Todd."

"Yes, sir."

It was thirty miles to Gettysburg, a good night's ride for

fresh men and horses, a cruel one for Stuart's cavalry in its fagged condition. But the leader did not hesitate. He knew he should have been with his commander two days before and he was sparing nothing to remedy the error as far as possible. So, weary, dirty and hungry as they were, they rode into the darkness without asking favors of fate.

To Hampton, who was fifteen years older but fully as tough as Stuart, was given the responsibility of bringing up the rear and prodding stragglers. Some of the horses had to be led to keep them on their feet. Many men were too tired to realize when they fell out of line. When a trooper went to sleep and slid to the ground, his mount stood beside him with drooping head until both were set in motion again by an officer. Where the officers found their endurance was a mystery to Ezra, but find it they did and, from the youngest lieutenant to the general himself, not one folded up.

"Suppose we would have more guts if we had taken our commissions when we had a chance?" Ezra mumbled to Fess.

"What's wrong with us as we be? We're here, hain't we? That's all can be said for the rest of 'em."

"I was never so tired in my life."

"That's the fault of the War Department, they should've issued cradles for the babies."

"You're a sympathetic old cuss!"

They ignored each other for the rest of the night. It seemed to Ezra that the earth had stopped turning and this side was stuck in eternal darkness. He wondered vaguely if the war would continue under that handicap, and when he realized what he was thinking about he could not decide whether he was awake or dreaming. It didn't make much difference. The column was still moving, hoofs shuffled in the dust, saddles creaked, sabers clattered against canteens, crickets fiddled along the roadside. Up there in the sky, or beyond it, the stars were still burning. Were there men on them, men riding their hearts out in the night to be on time to kill other men on the morrow?

On and on and on. July first became July second. The armies of Lee and Meade slept, but Jeb Stuart's cavalry did not rest. The slender, quiet man in gray needed them and they were coming. They reached him as the sun rose over the hot, misty fields around Gettysburg. Three days sooner, two days, perhaps one day, would have given the man a better chance. He knew it, but he did not chide them. He was too big to blame others for what they could not do.

For the moment, there was little scouting necessary. Both armies, after a full day's battle, knew approximately each other's strength and position. Stuart rode off to confer with Lee and Hampton told his men to rest. Most of them were soon asleep, but the general had no such thought. Always a hunter, with an eye for cover that might conceal game or enemies, he rode out in front of the line and sat studying a piece of woodland that stretched behind a rail fence. A bullet whined past his head and a rifle cracked in front of him.

It was characteristic of him that he neither retreated nor raised an alarm but drew his revolver and rode in to settle the matter alone. He spotted the sniper behind a tree and let fly, but the range was too great for a pistol. The Yankee shot again and put a bullet through Hampton's cape. The general galloped straight up to the fence and fired. The Federal's right arm dropped, shot through; he wheeled and disappeared among the trees.

Back in the line Fess heard the shots and sat up. Then he let out a yell that raised the regiment: "Look out, Gen'ral! Look out!" A Northern cavalryman had come out of nowhere, the turf muffling the sound of his horse's feet, and was driving home a saber cut at Hampton's unsuspecting head. The fact that the general and his horse were both unusually tall kept the blow from gathering sufficient momentum, otherwise he would have been felled. Surprised and half stunned, he wheeled and thrust his revolver almost in the man's face. The hammer just snapped. The Yankee saw he had stirred up a bear and rode for his life with Hampton after him, snapping the perverse pistol that missed fire every time. Finally the Federal dodged through an open barway into the woods. Hampton rose in his stirrups and, swearing in a voice that made the leaves tremble, hurled the revolver after him.

A dozen troopers ran out to help, but he would have none of them. There was a four-inch wound in the top of his head and blood was trickling into his beard, but most of all he was furious and continued to rave at the pistol while Dr. Taylor patched up his scalp. The men grinned and lay down again, well pleased that they had lived to see the day when the Old Man got mad enough to swear.

To Ezra and many others in Stuart's Division the rest of the day was a time of strange waiting. According to reports, the previous day's fighting had been a draw, and now it was raging again. They could see nothing of it, but south of their position rose the thunder of artillery and lesser sounds. To be sure, the outfit was dog-tired, but after a few hours' rest it could have gone into action. And it wanted to fight. A great battle was going on, Lee was outnumbered and needing every man he could muster, yet the cream of his cavalry sat there, out of the way, and waited.

In the afternoon there was a brush with Federal cavalry which seemed unimportant to those who took part in it. To Stuart and Hampton and their men who had tried so hard to get there, the second day of Gettysburg was a disappointment.

Though they went to sleep wondering what had happened on other parts of the field, the troopers put in a good night and were almost fresh in the morning. During that time Stuart learned that Gregg, the Federal cavalry leader, who had a reputation of being a busy and skillful fighter, was at large with six thousand men north of the main battle lines. That happened to be the same territory assigned to Stuart for the day's operations, the plan being for him to strike around the Union right whenever Lee could hit the center. Now Gregg must be found and disposed of, not only to clear the way but to prevent him from carrying out a similar maneuver against the Confederate infantry. So, early in the morning the long gray lines, no longer prancing but very businesslike, set out to hunt their quarry.

They rode through a beautiful country of little shady roads and farmlands where birds sang and wheat ripened and cattle grazed. For a while there was no sign of an enemy and it was hard to believe that not far off a hundred and fifty thousand men were trying to kill each other.

"This isn't a battle," Ezra said to Preston, as they paused on a knoll and looked down at a meadow where two farmers were drawing hay. "It's a dream."

"The Yankee roosters will wake us up." Preston smiled with his eyes the way his father did.

It was nearly two o'clock of a sweltering day when the two mounted forces found each other near where the Hanover and Low Dutch roads crossed. Gregg tried to land the first blow and the four Confederate brigades lined up to meet him —Fitzhugh Lee, Hampton, Chambliss and Jenkins. But there was faulty coordination among them. Already Lee and Hampton had misunderstood each other, and now Chambliss charged the center and found himself in trouble. Hampton took two regiments and galloped to his relief, intending to bail him out and straighten the line. However, in the excitement someone got the idea that a general advance had been ordered and the word ran through the ranks. Ezra, who had ridden ahead with Hampton, looked back as horizontal lightning flickered along the line—thousands of sabers came out and up—followed by the thunder of hoofs and a mighty yell.

They came on, wave after wave of galloping horses ridden by men who held their heads high, the brims of their slouch hats pushed back by the wind. Yankee batteries opened up on the left, right and center, backed by thousands of barking carbines. The gray squadrons absorbed the fire but did not falter. Horses went down and the flood poured over them, saddles showed suddenly empty and there was no trace of the riders who had filled them. The gaps closed, the sabers flashed, the lines bore down in a solid front.

Gregg's blue horsemen rode to meet them and the two columns crashed into each other with the noise of a dozen colliding freight trains. Horses were raised on end and fell over backward, men hurtled through the air and disappeared in the mass. The squadrons behind spread toward the wings, expanding the line and giving the troopers room to fight. A thousand saber duels raged simultaneously and the Southerners were surprised to find the Yankees were good when it came to hand to hand. Those farmers and merchants weren't supposed to go in for the aristocratic art of swordplay. Everyone fought madly with all he had: color-bearers used their spike-tipped staffs as lances; artillerymen swung their rammers when pistols failed or sabers broke; riders clinched and pitched from their saddles, biting, gouging and choking. North and South had boasted mightily of their mounted troops and now was the test.

Ezra had no clear idea of the battle; he was fighting so hard to keep his seat that as far as he was concerned the field was only a few yards in circumference. What little he knew about swordsmanship was forgotten and he acted intuitively, thrusting, slashing and parrying desperately to protect his own skin from one moment to the next. He tried to keep near the general, but wheeling, thrashing horses pushed him to one side. If a man ever went down in that crush he would be gone. Occasionally he heard Hampton's great voice roaring encouragement to the men and the sound seemed like a shield that kept death away.

There came a lull, or at least time for him to reload his revolver. He realized that the sun was cruelly hot and wondered if there was a drink left in his canteen.

"Ezra!" It was Fess' high-pitched voice, now almost a shriek. "The gen'ral! For Gawd's sake come on!"

Fess tore past him bareheaded, his shirt in ribbons, his sword rising and falling as he beat his horse with the flat of it. Ezra followed blindly—then he saw Hampton. Hemmed against a fence in a narrow lane, he was fighting alone against a crowd of Federals. His long sword flashed and one went down. He pulled his revolver and the Yanks drew back momentarily. Two of his troopers tried to reach him but were cut down. The Federals charged and he fired point-blank, dropping the first one. The others circled and closed in, slashing at his head. One landed a blow that made him reel, but he came back like a hickory sapling and all but cut off the fellow's head. The survivors drew off from the giant who had been a match for six men.

But Hampton was hard hit; blood was pouring down his forehead, into his eyes and dripping from his beard. Half blinded, he shook his head and fumbled with his revolver. The Federals rode in for the kill.

"We're comin', Wade!" Ezra screamed.

Not only were they coming, they arrived, hitting the three Northerners broadside. Standing in their stirrups, Fess and Ezra cut down two, while the third horse went down with its rider. Other Federals were riding up.

"Jump the fence, General!" Ezra yelled. "Quick! We'll hold 'em."

Two more Confederates galloped in and the four of them screened him. For once, he had had enough. Though reeling in his saddle, he was still the superb horseman as he wheeled his big mount and lifted him lightly over the fence. As he landed, Hampton nearly fell, for while in the air a splinter of shell had ripped into his side. The four troopers beat off the Yankees and rode back to where he sat, deathly pale and soaked with blood.

"I am out of it," he said weakly. "Tell Baker to take the command. Don't stop fighting."

With tears running down his face Fess put an arm around his old friend's shoulders and motioned Ezra to ride close on the other side. Slowly they helped him from the field and at a distance laid him down in a farm shed.

"I believe he will live," Dr. Taylor said that evening. "He has the strength of ten men."

A moment later Preston rode up. "Thank God for one favor," he said, when he heard.

"Only one?" Ezra asked.

"At the moment." Preston leaned against his horse. "The army is in retreat. General Lee has ordered us to protect the rear."

The battle of Gettysburg was over. The Confederacy was wounded unto death.

Chapter 15

IT RAINED throughout the night of July fourth. Like thousands of other wounded, General Hampton lay on the bare floor of a springless ambulance, a shattered fragment of Lee's broken army. The roads were rutted but the drivers kept their mules at the trot, for Federal cavalry would soon be in pursuit. The general's staff and a few other friends rode near him to stand together in one last fight if necessary. No one knew where the rest of the troops were and at the moment it did not matter. They had done their best, they were beaten, and their only hope was to put the Potomac between themselves and the enemy.

A lantern on the rear of the ambulance gave Ezra occasional glimpses of Fess' face. It was longer than ever and set in lines of fatigue and anxiety. He leaned against the rain, his head turned sideways to catch any sound from inside the vehicle. The general did not speak, but up and down the line pitiful voices were screaming, cursing and praying as the lurching wagons tore open unbandaged wounds and twisted broken bones. The cry of "Water!" sounded everywhere, mingled with the entreaties of men who wanted to be left to die beside the road and of others begging to be shot. The very marrow of Ezra's spine seemed frozen with horror, yet he could do nothing. Officers hurried the teams ahead. There was no time to fill canteens or adjust bandages or say encouraging words. The cold fingers of despair were at every man's throat and necessity took the form of brutality.

Morning came. The mules were still trotting; the men who rode beside the ambulance were specters, stiff with mud, so exhausted they could not raise their eyes to the sky. Preston dismounted, stumbling as he tried to run, and climbed into the wagon that carried his father. The others watched the tail-board for his reappearance.

"Lord!" Fess sobbed. "Iffen I only had a drink to send him!"

"He can't have lived through the night," Ezra said dully. "He was wounded three times."

"Damn the Yankees!" Fess' eyes were red in his white face. "Damn every one of 'em iffen they've killed Wade Hampton."

"Hush!"

Preston lifted the curtain in the rear of the wagon and dropped to the ground.

"He is alive—that is all," he said to the knot of soldiers.

"Conscious?" one of them asked.

"Yes. He says we mustn't let him be taken alive."

Preston remounted and they moved on. Horses were going down and the road was clogged with troopers on foot. On each side of the column they lay on the grass, sound asleep as they hit the ground. The mules had slowed to a crawl and no one objected; there was not enough energy to create impatience. Hart's Battery got stuck in the mud and was shouldered out by soldiers who used their last ounce of strength and sank in their tracks. Thus what was left of the Army of Northern Virginia crawled home.

There was nothing to eat for man or beast and nothing to

drink but roadside water. The cries of the wounded decreased as the men became exhausted or died. Troopers dozed in their saddles and teamsters slept on the wagon seats, sometimes pitching forward under the heels of mules too tired to kick. Only the indomitable officers kept the lines moving through the deepening mud.

"He is still living," Preston reported at noon. "He won't accept special attention, even if I could find a doctor. He will take his turn with the others."

"How far is it to the river?" Ezra asked.

"Perhaps fifteen miles—I don't know."

"Where is General Stuart?"

"I believe he is covering Lee and the main army. I don't know, Ezra, I don't know anything."

"If you can find a place to lie down in a wagon, I'll lead your horse."

"Thank you. I'll tough it out with the rest."

"Sprout offen the ol' tree," Fess muttered.

Toward sunset the clouds lifted, showing the Potomac swollen and angry as it swept past the town of Williamsport. As the straining column pressed forward to attempt the difficult crossing, troops of blue cavalry were sighted in the rear. It was not a mere patrol but full seven thousand horsemen with eighteen pieces of artillery. They were looking for General Lee and believed they had found him.

Groggy officers in gray became alert and prepared their defense with the cold skill of desperation. The ambulances were rushed toward the river and behind them a thin line began forming. Every man who could carry a gun was in that line: cooks, staff officers, orderlies and as many teamsters as could be spared. Some of the wagons stopped to allow wounded to join the ranks. Many of them, too weak to stand, were still able to shoot sitting down. There were perhaps two thousand all told, keystoned by Hart's Battery.

The Federals charged, but not with their usual zest, for they, too, were tired. There was not a break in the gray wall to encourage the horsemen and they wheeled back without coming to grips. Hart hurled shells after them and their field-pieces replied, but soldiers who had just passed through Gettysburg paid small attention to a handful of guns.

The sun was down and it was raining again. Those who could not stand sat in the mud, hanging onto ramrods and sticks to steady their aim when the next charge came. The ones on horseback could see the line of ambulances pushing into the river. A few were already across, proving that the ford was still passable.

The Federals came on once more, deploying to envelop the little force that they outnumbered more than three to one. But they never finished the maneuver, for, as usually happens only in stories, out of the twilight rode Jeb Stuart and three thousand troopers. The bluecoats turned and rode away, having had enough, and Stuart was too tired to follow. Then night came, and those who had fought so well and lost so much found rest on the friendly soil of Virginia.

Hampton spent two weeks in a hospital at Winchester before he was able to be moved home to South Carolina. They said he could not live, but he did. Then they said he would never fight again, and his answer to that was to report for duty on November third. By then he had been made a major general and commanded a division.

During his absence the cavalry had little respite. All summer Lee and Meade faced each other along the Rapidan, neither strong enough to attack. But the Union cavalry, especially the part of it under fox-faced Kilpatrick, was stronger every day and clashed repeatedly with Stuart between the lines. As the indefatigable Stuart had taken over Hampton's command, that division was in every possible engagement. There were no sustained battles, but many sharp encounters, the galloping, yelling kind in which the Southerners excelled and in which they were usually successful. To the hardened troopers on both sides those wild clashes were warfare at its best.

Although he was not yet twenty years old, Ezra was a man in experience and hardship. Sometimes, when he looked in a mirror, he was startled to see not the face of that boy who had stared pop-eyed at the sight of a soldier, but a weather-beaten visage set in purposeful lines. All he had experienced had given him no clearer concept of the war. Now, as at first, he was not fighting for the ideals of the Confederacy, even if he had understood them, but from loyalty to his friends. Since finding his uncle and acquiring something definite to hope for, the whole thing had become more distasteful and far less romantic.

The autumn of 1863 passed and the army went into winter quarters. Villages of huts and tents and dugouts appeared as before; they were as dirty and smoky and would soon be as vermin-ridden as ever, but their atmosphere was different.

During the period of rest, when there was time to take stock, it was plain that morale was low. The defeat at Gettysburg, the months of uncertainty that followed, and the knowledge that things were going badly for the Confederacy on other fronts, was beginning to tell on even the most heroic spirits.

Every soldier could, and most of them did, grumble openly about the way government officials handled things. The poor food was getting poorer, though letters from home proved there was plenty in the South. Thousands of tons of supplies rotted because the transportation system could not deliver it where it was needed. Justly or not, the army blamed this on political red tape.

It was the same with wages. When a man waited six months or a year for his eleven dollars a month and then found the money nearly worthless, he naturally said rough things about those who managed the nation's finances. So they grumbled and by the thousands refused to re-enlist or deserted outright, feeling that the war was being lost by stupid politicians and that a common man was justified in going home to take care of his family. General Lee was awake to the situation and with characteristic justice put his finger on the reasons for it: "Insufficiency of food and non-payment of the troops have more to do with the dissatisfaction than anything else."

Not that all the men sulked or that all the days were dreary. A majority of the soldiers still stuck to their original ideals and resolved to hang on until the tide turned. To do this they made the most of such fun as came within their reach. They put on theatricals and musicals, issued camp newspapers, played every possible game, and strained all imaginable excuses to get themselves invited to civilian parties far and near. It was when the snow came that they really went to town. Perhaps at no other time in all history has snowballing been practiced as scientifically as it was in those winter days. It was the great sport of the army, the time when all barriers were down and all men were boys again. West Pointers who had outdone the best Federal commanders put their heads together to plan the strategy of those snow battles. Entire regiments were used and manuevers were carried out with all the spirit of genuine combat. No punches were pulled. Stones and chunks of ice were at the core of the snowballs and the "wounded" were often just that, with teeth knocked out, black eyes and bloody noses.

There was plenty of room for troop movements and thousands of men stormed heights, fought for bridges, and defended communication lines. Officers whose names were at the top of the world's military roster led those troops. Hampton was in the thick of it and Longstreet won a battle by heading a charge and personally collaring the enemy commander. To the thoughtful it was a heartening demonstration of democracy at play.

Festival Jones, who was always pessimistic in winter because he hated cold weather, took a different view of those sham battles.

"Fun for young'uns but not fitten for men," he grumbled as he laboriously sewed a canvas patch on his only pair of pants. They were part of a Federal uniform "donated" by a prisoner.

"What's wrong with a little fun?" Ezra did not look up from greasing his dilapidated boots.

"Did you ever stop to think— Aow!" Fess pricked his thumb with the needle and swore freely.

"You need a pair of Jeb Stuart's elbow gauntlets lined with tin."

"Shut up!" Fess sucked his thumb, then spat in the fire. "As I was sayin', did you ever stop to think that a year ago we was raidin' behind the Yank lines most to Washin'ton, but now they're back of our lines? That damn Kilpatrick'd have burned Richmond 'n' murdered Jeff Davis iffen we hadn't rid all day in a snowstorm 'n' headed him off."

"But we did head him off!" Ezra held a boot over the fire. "And we got three hundred and fifty of his men and five hundred of his horses. What's so bad about that?"

"A year ago he wouldn't 'ave tried it that's the idee. We're slippin' down hill, bub. We're short of hosses 'n' men 'n' ever'thing. But the Yanks're buildin' up—they've even got britch-loadin' carbines."

"I'd rather have our muzzle-loaders—they shoot farther and harder."

"We couldn't git powder for them iffen we didn't take it from the Yanks."

"Oh, cheer up, Fess! We'll get on when spring comes."

A knock rattled on the door and a soldier stuck his head inside. "Orders for you, Ezra," he said. "Git over to Cap'n Stone's tent for Cook's court-martial."

"Heck!" Ezra threw a piece of firewood at the intruder who grinned and disappeared. "I don't want to testify, Fess."

"Got to. Cook deserves it, too. Wear my hat—it's got two less holes'n yourn."

When Ezra entered Captain Stone's quarters he found him sitting with Lieutenants White and Savery on camp stools and looking befittingly solemn. Across from them, under guard, stood Private Cook, dark and glowering. A minute later Lieutenant Wade of the provost guard came in.

"We will proceed," Stone announced, having been designated president of the court. "Lieutenant Savery, as judge advocate you will present the charge against the prisoner."

"Yes, sir." Savery stood up and read from a paper:

"Charge—conduct to the prejudice of good order and military discipline. Specification—in this that he, the said Private Cook of the 7th Company, did on the night of March 4, 1864, maliciously take for his own purposes a keg of wine designated and marked for hospital use.
                    (Signed) L. W. Savery, C.S.A.
                    Witness: Lieut. G. E. Wade
                    Pvt. Ezra Todd."

Lieutenant Savery looked hard at the prisoner and said, "Private Cook, you have heard the charge preferred against you. How say you, guilty or not guilty?"

"Not guilty," Cook answered sullenly.

"Private Todd, take the oath of a witness," Stone ordered.

"Yes, sir." Ezra was sworn in.

"Now give the court your reason for apprehending the prisoner."

"Yes, sir." Ezra thought a moment. "Last night from ten to twelve I did sentry duty for a sick friend. My post was behind the hospital, from the woods to the brook. I saw a bull's-eye lantern in the supply tent and investigated. Cook had a keg of wine on his shoulder. He tried to get away but I nabbed him and turned him over to the provost guard. That is the story, sir."

"Lieutenant Wade, take the oath," Stone directed.

"Yes, sir."

"Testify."

Wade, who was very tall and thin, nearly hit the canvas roof with his head when he straightened up.

"I was in command of the guard last night," he said. "At about eleven-fifteen Private Todd brought in Private Cook for the reason you have just heard. I put Cook under arrest and went back with Todd. The keg of wine was where he said it was, about ten paces from the supply tent. We returned it to the tent. That is all, sir."

"What have you to say, Cook?" Captain Stone demanded.

"Sure, I tried to lug it off." Cook glared at one after another. "Why not? I was cold and I was hungry. We don't have half enough rations nor no money to buy more with. The wine was there doin' nobody no good. If Todd was a man he wouldn't have squealed on me."

"Wait a minute," Ezra put in. "Were you ever in a hospital?"

"No," Cook snapped.

"Well, I have been and I know if there are any extras goin' round the boys in the hospitals should have 'em. If you were a man you wouldn't think of stealing from your sick comrades."

"I'll knock hell out of you, some day!" Cook roared.

"Order in the court!" Stone said sternly. "Is there any more testimony?"

There was none, at least none fit to be aired there. The three officers went to the back of the tent and conferred in low tones, then Captain Stone came back with the verdict. It was that Cook was to do sentry duty six hours of each day for thirty days, the time and place of such duty being left to the discretion of his company commander. And, the captain paused before he laid it on, one hour of each day he must stand on a wine keg like the one he had attempted to steal, exposed to public view with a placard marked THIEF in three-inch letters hanging from his neck. The court was dismissed.

Ezra disliked making enemies, but this incident gave him no regret, because the soldier deserved his punishment. No doubt Cook had been cold and miserable—everyone was more or less—but he was much better off than the ones he had planned to rob. If that was all the honor he had, he had better have walked out some night and let the army profit by his absence. His kind always stuck around hoping to pick up a safe and easy living. Between battles they stole anything they could eat, drink or sell, and when the fighting started they managed to get "lost" until it was over. Ezra had seen several such drummed out of camp and he wished all of them might get as much or more.

A few days later he came in from carrying a message to Stuart. When he had rubbed his horse down he left the picket line and walked through the woods at the edge of camp. Winter had disappeared like a whipped wolf and the whole world was astir with the business of spring.

"How are the roads, Todd?" Lieutenant Wade stepped from among the trees.

"Roads?" Ezra grinned but did not salute, for such formalities were usually ignored in everyday camp life. "There ain't a road to be seen—just streams of mud."

"Any news at headquarters?"

"Nothing much. The Yanks have a new top man—U. S. Grant."

"So?" Wade raised his eyebrows. "Pretty good according to reports—Shiloh, Vicksburg, you know."

"And he's brought a feller named Sheridan to take over the cavalry. Old Kilpatrick has been sent west to Sherman. Looks like we gave him his belly full."

Wade smiled. "I reckon Marse Robert will give a get-acquainted party for the newcomers before long."

As they talked Ezra glanced toward the log cabin that was used for a regimental guardhouse. A sentry stood at the door and, after a second look, Ezra observed, "I see you have our old friend Mr. Cook working out his time."

Wade nodded. "Might as well have him doing something useful."

"Who's the prisoner?"

"A Yank the boys picked up last night. He goes to Belle Isle in the morning."

As Ezra passed the guardhouse he noticed a face pressed against the barred window but thought nothing about it. He dried out by the cabin fire and was beginning to think of supper when a trooper came in.

"The Yank in the guardhouse wants to talk with you, Ezra," he said. "He saw you go by and asked your name because you look so much like somebody he knowed up north. Thinks you must be kin."

"What's his name?"

"Didn't say. Got any Yankee crackers left?"

"Two boxes. Can you use one?"

"Can I! Mister, I hain't et for two days."

"Take this box. Thanks for the message, though I think it's fishy."

He slipped a pistol into his pocket and went out into the twilight, wondering if the prisoner could be his uncle or some other member of his lost family. It didn't sound like Captain Marsh, yet it was possible. When he came to the guardhouse, inside which a candle was burning, he saw that Cook was still on duty.

"The Yank sent for me?" Ezra asked, as though nothing had happened between them.

"Yeh. Want to go in?" Cook's voice was not unfriendly.

"May as well."

Cook raised the bar and Ezra stepped inside. He saw no one for a moment, then Bert Sears lunged at him with a knife. As Ezra reached for his pistol a million stars danced before him, then darkness came.

Chapter 16

EZRA'S next thought was that his head was the size of the captive balloon he had seen outside of Richmond and that it was bursting at the seams. The pain spread as consciousness returned, until it included his left shoulder and arm. Obviously he had caught a terrific glancing blow from behind, probably from a club or rifle butt. Thank heaven it had been glancing.

It had happened not long before, because the candle set in a bottle looked about the same height. He tried to sit up and found that his left side was pinned down. Feeling around with his other hand, he discovered that a knife had been driven between his arm and ribs through his shirt and deep into the floor. He pulled it out and sat up. He felt dizzy but his mind was working clearly. Or perhaps it didn't have to be in perfect condition to figure out that Cook and Bert had ganged up on him. Two of a kind—trust them to get together if there was any dirty work afoot. Each wanted to kill him and each thought he had done so, but in the excitement and poor light Cook had struck to one side and Bert had not realized the the knife missed by a whisker's breath.

Of course both men escaped. By the time Ezra could walk and call the guard it was dark and search was useless.

"Better see a doctor," Wade advised.

"To thunder with a doctor!" Ezra snorted. "No bones are broken."

"Sure you feel all right, bub?" Fess asked anxiously. "Sometimes them things hang fire."

"Feel all right! Naturally I don't feel all right." Ezra raged. "I'm rarin', tearin' mad to think I was fool enough to let those yellow-bellied polecats put it over on me!"

"Take it easy, Todd, take it easy," Wade soothed.

"I'll never take it easy—never till I get Bert Sears. The next time he won't get away."

"He's purty handy at it," Fess commented.

"Oh, keep still!" Ezra roared. "If you laugh at me I'll beat the fog out of you, the way I feel right now."

"Come on, Spot." Fess snapped his fingers. "The gen'man's a mite riled. Me 'n' you'll git along home 'n' cook that rabbit you fetched in this afternoon."

Such personal incidents were soon tossed aside in the savage rush of war. The Confederacy was losing ground everywhere except in Virginia. There Lee and Grant faced each other in or near that great gloomy land of trees and rivers known as the Wilderness. To Ezra, as to many others, that word became synonymous with nightmare, in which such names as Spottsylvania and Cold Harbor stood out with horrible vividness.

Unable to get a clear idea of the country or what the various commanders were trying to do, he saw only a picture of tragic confusion. The roads and paths traveled night and day during those days in early May seemed to begin and end nowhere. They were only passageways through endless forests, sometimes clogged with moving troops and often obscured by smoke from burning underbrush where the wounded screamed in the fires. Again at night he rushed through the nothingness when the armies lay exhausted, so quiet that the whippoorwills dared to sing.

For Ezra the last shred of romance was forever gone from warfare. In that gloomy hell he found the ultimate of its stupidity. The generals blundered, issued new orders, and blundered again. Blue and gray regiments, the finest men on earth, sought each other in the murky tangle, got lost and were cut down by their own artillery. When they met they fought like fiends, yet if one side prevailed it struggled on without knowing where it was going.

The only humane elements were the medical units of North and South which, often working together, carried such wounded as they could find out to the roads where they lay in rows, the prey of thirst and mosquitoes, waiting for the ambulances that were long in coming. Burial squads moved in where the fighting had been hottest. Yanks and Johnnies borrowed shovels from each other, shared canteens, and swapped jokes. More of such sane comradeship in the beginning and they would have been unnecessary.

Despite his association with Hampton's headquarters, Ezra could not make out whether they were fighting one battle or a series of them. Preston, the optimist, assured him that General Lee knew exactly what he was doing.

"You see," Preston said one evening as they watered their horses at a brook, "Grant is scared. He is trying to break off the battle by a pretended thrust at Richmond. But we know he has sent only ten thousand cavalry under Sheridan."

"Only ten thousand!" Ezra looked up from where he was sitting on the bank. "That wild man Sheridan, with a force that size, can do a lot of damage."

"Oh, he won't go far." Preston never seemed tired or doubtful. "Jeb Stuart has taken the Divisions of Fitz Lee and Rooney Lee and gone after him. Too bad he didn't take us, but Marse Robert wants father here with him. Jeb will get Sheridan's scalp. I'll bet you ten dollars he is back with it before the middle of the month. Take me?"

"No. I haven't had ten dollars in ten months." Ezra looked into the water. "And I don't know how long it is to the middle of this month. What is today? I've lost track."

"May ninth." Preston smiled indulgently. "You need a nap, young fellow."

"Who doesn't?" Ezra got up and led his horse away.

Three days later he was waiting outside Hampton's tent, as he always did when in camp. There were no orders to that effect but he had a feeling that the general expected him to be there. He heard the familiar measured stride as the general walked up and down inside. He had been walking since the arrival and departure of a rider half an hour before.

"Ezra."

The lad jumped up and saluted. Hampton stood in the tent door, the turned-up ends of his sweeping mustache quivering. "Our beloved commander, General Stuart, is dead."

"Dead, sir!" Ezra felt cold. That gay little daredevil could not be dead.

"Yes. He was shot in battle at Yellow Tavern yesterday. He died in Richmond this morning."

"Did he stop Sheridan first, sir?" Ezra asked.

"Yes." Hampton turned and re-entered the tent.

The death of Stuart left Hampton as Lee's ranking cavalry commander. Promotion would not be official for several months by reason of politics, but that made little actual difference. He took over during the fateful hour when the tide turned definitely against the Army of Northern Virginia, as it had already turned against the other Southern forces. Stuart had been great in success; he loved it, and probably died happier than he would have a month later. Now his friend was given the heavier burden of carrying on in defeat but keeping untarnished the bright honor of Southern horsemen.

One of Hampton's first moves was to train his men to double as infantry. The troopers grumbled, for they scorned foot soldiering, but the general ignored their protests. It was not from lack of sympathy; simply, he had no illusions as to how things were going. For months it had been impossible to replace worn-out horses and already nearly two thousand of his cavalrymen were dismounted for that reason. This number was bound to grow, for the South could meet only a fraction of the demands of its armies, while the North was strong enough to repel the kind of raids that once yielded so many horses and other spoils. Hampton knew his cause was doomed but he had no intention of abandoning it. When his horses were gone he would fight on foot as long as he had a man to follow him.

The Wilderness campaign dragged its bloody trail across the month of May. At Cold Harbor, Grant suffered sixty

thousand casualties and the dead of both sides lay unburied
for days. The commanders deplored this butchery but could
not stop it. They were caught in a storm they could not control and must ride it out as best they could until it spent itself.
I pray for peace, Hampton wrote his wife at this time. *I
would not give peace for all the military glory of a Bona-
parte.*

But there was no peace. The cavalry was constantly in
action; by day they fought skirmishes that would have been
called battles earlier in the war, while at night they scouted
and did picket duty. So well did they learn to maneuver on
foot that more than once the Federals fell back, believing the
riders had infantry support. The swamps and brambles were
hard on shoes and uniforms and the survivors of the natty old
legion could scarcely believe their eyes when they looked at
their rags and bare feet. But the spirit was still there. Week
after week they fought weather, sickness, mosquitoes and
Yankees, on rations that had dwindled until three meals were
less than one had been.

By mid-June they had outridden and outfought Sheridan,
Gregg, Custer, and a dozen other top-notch Federal officers.
They had taken two thousand prisoners and considerable
supplies, but had lost more than seven hundred men, and
their horses were in heartbreaking condition. General Lee
was in no position to reward those heroic divisions, but on
July second he showed his appreciation by recommending
Hampton for the post of Chief of Cavalry. On August
eleventh the appointment was officially confirmed. The general accepted with no sign of pride. With all his heart he

hated war and for him there was only duty, no glory, in its pursuit.

About this time one thing gave him considerable satisfaction. Sheridan was moved from the Army of the Potomac to the Shenandoah Valley. Grant did not say so, but rumor had it he was ashamed of the way the little Irishman had been handled by Stuart and Hampton. Though always outnumbered, they had beaten him at every turn and given him nearly six thousand casualties in four months. So he was sent away to a safer place. Lee wanted to unleash Hampton on his trail, but every man was needed to keep Grant out of Richmond.

The cavalry's main job was scouting and breaking up the many thrusts by which the Federals were feeling out Lee's lines. Grant was wary of the gray troopers and kept his own mounted troops near home, so there was a lull in cavalry battles during September. Rest was welcome to the weary Confederates, but they still had to eat and food was scarcer every day. When Hampton's scouts told him the enemy had three thousand beeves corraled only thirty-five miles away he determined to try for them.

To pass undetected through the Federal lines to a point only five miles from their headquarters and return with that number of slow-moving cattle was no easy undertaking. Every mile of the way had to be mapped, enemy troop concentrations located, and preparations made to meet any emergency that might crop up. Hampton worked fast and secretly with his scouts, at the same time choosing twenty-seven hundred of his best mounted men and four guns for the job. Early in the morning of September fourteenth they quietly pulled out of camp near Petersburg, swung around south, and rode all day, camping that night at Wilkinson's Bridge. Only a few of the officers understood what was afoot, but the atmosphere was tense, for by then everyone knew they were behind the Union lines.

"What sort of raid is this, Todd?" a soldier asked, as they sat around eating cold rations, for fires were forbidden. "You must know, being thick with the staff crowd."

"I'm not in on it," Ezra told him, "but I don't think the general expects a battle—he looks too happy."

"I hope there's food in it for us," the man said. "Lord, I'm hungry! So's my hoss. The poor critter was gnawin' bark offen a hickory tree when I left him."

At daybreak they headed north, riding fast and with little noise until they came to Cook's Bridge on the Blackwater.

"Judas priest!" Fess growled, looking down the road. "The bridge is busted. The Old Man didn't count on that."

"Fall out and let this column pass," an officer ordered behind them.

As they pulled into the ditch Lieutenant Lannau, one of the engineers, and forty men trotted by with pioneer tools strapped to their saddles.

"Guess he did know it," Fess muttered with satisfaction.

Pickets were thrown out at close intervals with orders to pick up anyone who came along, for Hampton was taking no chances on betrayal. While the bridge builders worked, soldiers spread to nearby fields and dug sweet potatoes. There were still no fires, but a raw potato is not bad when one is hungry enough. The General ate his with the others while he rode about keeping an eye on everything, especially the distant road where a cloud of dust might be expected.

The bridge was mended by dark, but the troops did not cross until midnight, for it was only ten miles to Coggin's Point where the cattle were. The gun wheels were swathed in corn sacks and conversation was forbidden. The night was dark and warm, with enough breeze to cover the necessary sounds of moving columns. Farmers along the way slept or, if they heard the horses, gave no alarm; it was a common sound.

About three o'clock Hampton gave the men a rest at a crossroads, then divided his forces, sending one brigade left and one right while he kept straight on. At five o'clock the prize was in sight—long pens full of fat steers. To the half-starved Confederates it was a glimpse of heaven. They charged with a hungry yell, sabers out and spurs digging. The cattle guard, cavalry from the District of Columbia, tumbled out of its tents, fell back a short distance, and rallied behind fences and wagons. The raiders swept over them, slashing and shooting.

"Surrender!" Hampton roared at a half-dressed officer who stood with bare feet wide apart, a pistol in each hand.

"Go to hell!" the Yank retorted and blazed away.

The bullets missed Hampton but dropped Ezra's horse to its knees. As it rolled over dead, Ezra jumped clear and was knocked down by a riderless horse. Partly stunned, he reached out and felt a man on the ground, rubbed the dust out of his eyes and recognized the trooper he had talked with two nights before.

"Hit or had your wind knocked out?" he panted.

"Hit," the man answered.

"I'll get you out of here."

The fight had eddied to one side and Ezra dragged the soldier under a wagon where he would be safe from trampling.

"You were wrong, Todd, about not having a fight this time."

"It's most over. The boys are coming up from both sides."

"Don't forget me when you leave."

"I won't."

Ezra caught a loose horse and re-entered the action, which now consisted of rounding up prisoners, horses and other booty. The cattle pens were open and the steers were trotting down the road, guided by their new owners. Teams were hitched to wagons and the dead and wounded loaded in. Ten of the raiders had been killed and forty-seven injured—the battle had been hot while it lasted. When they were ready to move, the guns fell in behind and the column was off for home.

And they got there. News of the raid was carried to Federal headquarters outside Petersburg at the very moment Lee put on a nicely timed diversion there. Grant was away and his staff was not sure what was happening. Before they found out, two million pounds of beef on the hoof were where they were most needed. It was estimated there was enough to feed Lee's whole army for a month. Obviously the new Chief of Cavalry had not lost his cunning as a raider.

After that they had days of rest and feasting, a heavenly time when the smell of roasting, frying and boiling beef filled the air. It freshened in them the memories of home when good food was taken for granted and men ate like gentlemen, not like tramps. But they still looked like tramps, unbarbered and dirty. Especially dirty, for they had seen no soap in months.

Then someone had an idea. There was plenty of oak and hickory bark to burn for lye and now they had grease. It was easy when so many were willing to help, and soon they were making hundreds of pounds of soap a day. Clothes were boiled and scrubbed free of dirt and vermin, razors and scissors went to work, and if the regiments did not actually shine at least they had a more wholesome look. Even Spot had a bath, perhaps the only absent dog in the world to receive such attention.

This tranquillity could not last long. Grant, the bulldog, would not give up. And why should he? For every man he lost and every round he fired, two more were sent down from the north. Stop him in one place and he would break out in another through the thinning Confederate lines. He was pressing hard on Richmond and the men in gray and butternut brown were fighting their hearts out against growing odds.

By the middle of September Hampton's veterans were not only scouting and picketing, but fighting dismounted in the trenches. Many others had swallowed their pride and joined the infantry, for it was impossible to keep them supplied with horses. By the end of October, Grant was strong enough to launch two simultaneous attacks on Petersburg, the key to the capital.

On the right, Hampton's outposts were pushed back two miles by infantry and six thousand cavalry. General Hill put two divisions in motion to meet them, but it would take time to get there. Hampton, heavily outnumbered as usual, was the only one on hand and he did not hesitate. Dismounting his men along the little stream of Gravelly Run, he sent Hart and his battery across the bridge to better positions on the other bank. The Federals were good fighters and they came on, knowing what it might mean if they broke the line. The dismounted troopers were holding to a man, but the general knew there was a limit to their strength.

"Preston!" he shouted. But Preston, tired of staff duty, had joined the men on foot.

"Ezra!" the general roared. Firing on one knee behind a tree, Ezra heard him above the noise, jumped on his horse and reported. "Tell Hart to hold the bridge at all costs. Richmond may depend on it."

"Yes, sir!" Ezra bent over his horse's neck and dug in his spurs.

The gallant Hart needed no special orders. When Ezra reached him, he was aiming one of the guns that were firing point-blank at a hundred and fifty yards range. He nodded, when Ezra shouted the message in his ear, but did not stop what he was doing. Somewhere he had found sixty teamsters, armed them with muskets, and sent them crawling toward the bridge. Bullets pelted the battery but the gunners seemed to brush them off. When a man doubled up and pitched for ward Ezra leaped down and took his place passing ammuni tion. Hart smiled at him.

The men held. Federal artillery was feeling for the position; two horses of a gun team were killed by a cannon ball and then a caisson exploded. Hart looked over his shoulder at the wounded men, staggered, and fell sideways, catching at the wheel of a gun carriage. One leg stuck out at an unusual angle, all but shot away below the knee.

"Quick! That canteen over there!" Ezra shouted to the nearest gunner.

The man caught up the canteen and cut the cord that was attached to it in place of a strap. They rigged a tourniquet above Hart's knee and twisted it with a broken swab stick.

"We'll take him back," Ezra said.

Hart opened his eyes and shook his head. "Hold the bridge," he ordered.

"He's my commander." The man hesitated.

"He's not mine. Help me shoulder him."

They got him on Ezra's back and he left the field with Hart. Minutes seemed like hours before he reached a road and saw a freight wagon lumbering along.

"Hey! This man needs attention," he shouted to the driver.

"Yeh? I ain't a doctor."

"Take him to the nearest dressing station."

"Shore. I'll give you a hand with him. Quite a battle!"

When Ezra returned to the battery he found that Young's Brigade had come up and the bridge was secure for the time being. He made his way back to Hampton and reported.

"The best ones are dropping fast," the general said grimly. "Wade"—he turned to his son—"will you find Preston and remind him he is a staff officer. I require his services."

"Yes, sir." Wade gathered up his reins. "You know Preston always finds an excuse to be in the front line."

Hampton held out until midafternoon when reinforcements arrived. But holding was not enough; the enemy must be driven back from his threatening position, so a counterattack was launched. The center was formed of dismounted troopers protected by cavalry on both sides. By then a cold rain was falling. As the ranks fell in, the general pulled up just behind the first one in order to watch the field at that critical time. Then he saw Preston waving his hat and leading the charge on horseback, an outstanding target for Yankee riflemen. Hampton smiled proudly as any father would. His lips stiffened as Preston pitched headlong to the ground.

Young Wade was first to reach his brother. As he knelt beside him a bullet struck him in the back and he fell on his face. Hampton galloped up and swung to the ground. On his knees between his stricken sons, he raised Preston in his arms and kissed him. "Oh, my boy!" he sobbed as tears ran down his face. Preston tried to speak but could not.

Another staff officer fell.

"My Gawd, Gen'ral, git outen here!" Fess yelled, tearing up and swinging his horse broadside to shield the group. "The bastards're aimin' to git you all."

"Find Dr. Taylor," Hampton said, still holding Preston and trying to examine Wade.

"Yes, sir," an officer answered, falling as he spoke.

"I'll find him." Ezra dashed away.

He came upon the doctor sitting in a spring wagon that he used for a mobile operating table and brought him back at a gallop. By the time they had stretched Preston in the wagon, Wade had been helped onto a horse and led off the field. General Hampton rode beside the wagon, never taking his eyes from his dying son's face. The cold rain drove through the gathering darkness. He heard his men cheering and knew the battle was won.

Chapter 17

GENERAL HAMPTON was not one to mourn openly, even for his favorite son. Thousands of other boys had gone the same way and countless others were maimed for life. South and North, plans and dreams and families were shattered. Those were the things that grieved him year after year. In a letter to his wife he showed that his heartache was not only for his personal loss. *After every fight* [he wrote] *there comes to me an ominous paper marked "casualties," "killed" and "wounded." Sad words which carry anguish to so many hearts.* He put away the letters of sympathy from Jefferson Davis, Robert E. Lee, and hundreds of other friends, and went on with his work, quieter, more grim, more resolute than before. The depth of his wound was revealed unintentionally in an order that directed young Wade, as soon as he recovered, to return to Johnston's army. He could not endure the thought of another son being killed before his eyes.

So back to picketing and skirmishing. November came in, cold and dreary, and every man in Lee's army feared the winter more than the hordes of Grant. Though shelters against the cold were more essential than ever, they were fewer than in previous years because materials were scarcer and there was less energy. The army was sick and starving, worn out in body and soul. The men left bloody tracks on the frosty ground and had only dreamy memories of the time when they were not hungry. During the destructive campaigns of summer and fall they had lost what few cooking utensils they once owned. They now prepared their dwindling rations of corn meal and meat on turtle shells, flat stones and slabs of wood. In the cavalry they tried to crush their horse corn between stones and eat it raw, but it made their mouths ore and caused agonies of indigestion. There was still plenty of food in the South but the broken-down facilities of packing and transportation could not deliver it to the troops. What did get through was often spoiled; the potatoes were rotten, the beef was blue and slimy, the hardtack vermin riddled. So it was corn meal and bacon endlessly, until the soldiers hated it, although there was not enough of it in a week to meet the needs of a day.

The officers could do little to help their men or themselves. They might, and did, complain bitterly to the government, but it had small effect. They tried to purchase supplies from local farmers who refused to sell because Confederate money was all but worthless. Earlier in the war many officers had paid out of their own pockets, but now those pockets were empty. The men were badly off, yet the officers fared worse because they had lost more. Still they fought on, for the breaking point had not yet been reached.

There came a dour evening in November when the cold, damp air found every hole in ragged uniforms and fairly rattled the bones underneath. Ezra kicked open the door of the hut and stamped inside, where Fess sat cross-legged beside the stove they had made from a cracked iron kettle.

"The general says there's nothing more for us to do tonight." Ezra almost touched the tiny blaze with his red hands that were scabby with grime, for the soap was gone again.

"That all he said?" Fess looked up, chewing his cud of tobacco.

"Yes. Why?"

"Thought he might've mentioned rations. We was promised three goober nuts apiece. Or was it three for the regiment?"

"You're lucky to see the funny side of it, Fess. The general doesn't call it a joke. He doesn't have any more than we do."

"I know it, bub, I know it. Genuine officers don't. Only whippersnapper politicians're cossets. Feller told me that Lee himself's been livin' on rice for a month past."

"I'm going through the lines tonight," Ezra said abruptly. "I may pick up a chicken or something. Coming with me?"

"The Yanks've grabbed ever'thing. They don't have to steal but they like to."

"I'm going to see." Ez turned toward the door.

"Hold on! I'll go 'long to look after you. Four years ago Hampton told me to keep an eye on you 'n' the orders hain't been changed."

"A lot has happened in those four years, Fess. A war has been fought—or most of it has."

"Yeh, 'n' a squirt of a boy has growed into a man who'd be fairly good-lookin' iffen he had a bath 'n' some clo'es 'n' two ounces uv meat on his bones."

"If is a big word sometimes."

"What you goin' to do when the war's over, bub?"

"I've told you about my uncle. There are times when I

almost wish I could desert and go to New York and look up
my family and get a square meal— Oh, well! I suppose you
still plan to go back to Cashier's Valley."

"Yeh, 'n' never come out agin. Jest fish 'n' hunt 'n' farm
a little, 'n' eat all I can hold every day. Sound good?"

"Wonderful. But right now there's something else to do.
Ready?"

"Yeh." Fess picked up his rifle and made a backward motion
with one hand. "You can't go, Spot. Damn Yanks might shoot
you."

They went out in the darkness and paused a moment to
get the set of the wind. The camp was unusually quiet and
Ezra remembered poignantly how Jeb Stuart and Preston
used to sing. Gone! No matter what happened now, those
voices and many others had taken with them some precious
thing the South would never know again.

"Come on, come on!" Fess urged.

They went down to the stream, where a picket told them
he had heard no sound of enemy patrols. The water was half
up to their knees and seemed warmer than the air until they
came out on the other side, when the cold threatened to cut
the legs from under them. They stood on the bank listening,
then moved up carefully into the bushes that fringed a road.
The smell of pine smoke was noticeable, then the measured
tramp of a man on the frozen clay. The footsteps nearly died
out, then returned, and faded in the other direction. The
sound of two voices drifted back as the sentries paused for
a word together.

Fess squeezed Ezra's arm and they crossed the road, planting each foot carefully before putting weight on it. The picket was coming again and passed down and back not a dozen feet from where they stood in the scrub pine. When he was gone they went into an open field that felt like a pasture in the darkness. Perhaps ten rods beyond was a campfire and four Yankees toasting food on long sticks.

"Fire 'n' grub," Fess whispered wistfully.

"Come along." Ezra poked him in the back.

There was no other fire visible so they moved on through the field, while the north wind blew colder and pellets of icy snow began falling, clicking as they hit stones and gun barrels.

"I never was so cold in my life," Ezra muttered.

"Want to go back?"

"There must be a farm around here. I want some milk or eggs or a hen or something."

"Iffen there's a live hen out tonight she's wearin' fur stid of feathers."

"There's a light, Fess! In a house, too."

"Mebbe Gen'ral Grant's headquarters. We'll make a call."

They reconnoitered the place and found it unguarded even by a dog. It was only a cabin but it was snug and an old gentleman and a lady sat by a dancing fire.

"I can't stand it!" Ezra almost wept. "I'm going in there and ask to warm up. Coming?"

"It hain't jest the thing to do, seein' we're surrounded by blue-bellies." Fess hesitated, looking through the window at the fire. "Yeh, I'll go."

Ezra rapped on the door and was invited in without question. The old couple still sat by the fire and seemed not at all surprised by the appearance of their callers.

"Sir," Ezra explained, "we are wet and cold. May we dry out here?"

"By all means." The man smiled at his wife, who nodded. "Do you remember, Mary, when we were in a similar predicament in Switzerland, how grateful we were to the cottagers who took us in?" She nodded again.

Who these unusual people were and how they happened to have been in Switzerland did not matter; they had a fire and the willingness to share it, which was enough. The two soldiers stood their rifles in a corner, pulled off their boots and stretched out on the hearth so that their wet feet steamed in the heat.

"This may not be heaven but it's near enough." Ezra sighed luxuriously.

"I am sure we possess no celestial attributes." The old man smiled at his wife.

"Prob'ly the Yanks lugged 'em off," Fess remarked. "They steal ever'thing."

"On the contrary, we find them very considerate neighbors," the old man said.

Fess pretended to stretch languidly and his hand closed over a small piece of bread that had perhaps dropped in the edge of the ashes during supper. Lazily the arm flexed, he yawned behind his hand and the bread was gone.

After a minute the host remarked to his wife, "My dear, do you remember how hungry we were that night in Switzerland? The peasants gave us milk, cheese and bread." She nodded. "It is possible that our friends would relish similar fare." He glanced at Fess and raised his eyebrows inquiringly.

"Mister"—Fess leaned forward—"do you mean are we hungry?"

"It occurred to me you might be."

"We have no money to pay for food, sir," Ezra put in.

"And we have no food to sell." The man nodded to his wife who returned the nod and left the room.

When she came back she had been transformed, in the eyes of the two soldiers, into an angel bearing on a wooden tray a tall pitcher of milk, tin cups, two great loaves of bread and two wedges of cheese.

"My lord!" Ezra whispered, tears smarting in his eyes.

"Remember your manners, bub," Fess said aside. They bowed their heads for a moment in silence.

While they ate, the clouds that had pressed so closely upon their world lifted and were dissipated in a clear, peaceful sky. An hour before, the weight of the war had seemed crushing, but now their spirits stood up again, breathed, and felt strong. With good food under their belts and warmth in their veins they were overcome by contentment and dozed as the fire crackled.

"Hands up!"

They jerked awake and saw a Federal captain in the doorway, backed by several men.

"It is customary to knock before entering," the old man said indignantly.

"Not in wartime, Grandpa. We looked through the window

and saw you harboring these rebels. That is a serious offence," the officer said severely.

"A higher authority than your commander once said, it is good to feed the hungry."

"We won't argue about it. Come on, you Johnnies. General Lee is going to miss you."

"Let him." Fess scowled. "I've toted a gun for him nigh four years 'n' I'm plumb sick 'n' tired of it."

"That's talking." The captain turned to Ezra. "Do you feel the same way, Reb?"

"No." Ezra glared at Fess. "I'll fight as long as there is a Yankee left."

"Which may be quite a while yet," the captain said good-naturedly. "Tie 'em up, boys, we must be on our way."

Resistance would have been stupid, unarmed as they were and outnumbered six to one. Their hands were tied and they were marched down the road to where the Federals' horses waited. There they were helped into saddles and put in line, each of their mounts led by a cavalryman. Wherever they might be going it would not be a pleasant ride, for the wind was bitter and snow was falling.

Fess talked incessantly, as a man will who has broken under strain and doesn't care what he says. He raged against the war, cursed the army and the whole Confederate government for a pack of fools and scoundrels. Ezra listened in amazement, then in anger, for even though the man had obviously reached the limit of endurance that was not sufficient excuse for stabbing those who had not. He had known Fess for years and these were the first disloyal words he had ever heard him speak. Perhaps he was insane; many soldiers were taken that way. Whatever the cause, Ezra realized that Fess was no longer dependable.

"I hate the hull kit 'n' bilin' of the lousy corn-bread mixers!" he ranted to the captain. "Give me grub, give me clo's, give me a gun 'n' I'll show you which side I'm on. I'll show you what I think of the Confed'rate States of Ameriky!"

"Hush up!" Ezra shouted at him. "You have no business talking that way."

"You peak-nosed fool!" Fess squeaked in his highest voice. "I've sweat 'n' froze 'n' starved 'n' earnt the right to say what I please. I've wanted to say it for a long time 'n' now I'm sayin' it while I'm amongst folks who won't shoot me for it. 'N' you can't run 'n' tattle to the officers, you white-livered ape!"

The soldiers laughed and Ezra rode in silence, thinking furiously. Soon he thoughts centered on his hands, which ached wickedly.

"Captain," he called out, "my hands are freezing. If you don't untie them you'll have a case of frostbite to answer for."

"I suppose that could happen," the officer agreed. "Give me your word to stay put?"

"Yes, sir."

"Cut him loose, boys."

"Thank you, sir."

It was better after that. The cold was unpleasant but there was no danger of freezing.

"Take your feet out of the stirrups and let the blood run down into your toes," said the man next to him.

"I learned that years ago, but you're quite decent to tell me."

"I always feel sorry for Johnnies, they're so soft."

"General Grant doesn't think so."

"Sure he does. He tells us to fetch in as many as we can of the poor hungry critters."

"Nice of him."

"I hear your folks don't send you much grub."

"They don't have to, ours comes from Washington."

"And your clothes, Johnny, they're shameful."

"Do you think we wear our best clothes when we go out to kill hogs?"

The soldiers laughed but Fess shouted angrily, "Shut up, bub! That hain't no way to talk to friends."

"Friends!" Ezra snorted.

"Yes, friends. They'll feed us, which is more 'n' the Jeff Davis gang'll do."

Ezra made no reply to this new Festival Jones. They trotted fast for an hour on a road that must lead to the James River. After a while campfires spread on both sides, revealing long rows of tents and lines of supply wagons drawn up in neat rows. The Federals were good soldiers and even fleeting glimpses in the night showed them going about their business with skill and confidence.

Ezra judged it was short of midnight when they came to the river and saw the lights of many ships tied up along the shores. After a few words with the captain, a snappy provost guard took over the prisoners and marched them down the bank and into a skiff in which they were rowed across the river to what looked to be a barge. There they were separated, Fess going one way and Ezra another.

"In here, Johnny," a guard said, holding his lantern up to an open door on deck.

"What sort of place is this?" Ezra asked casually.

"Temporary quarters till you get your ticket north. In you go. We'll send you some blankets pretty soon."

"Thank you, Yank."

"Don't mention it. We just love to take care of you Johnnies." He closed the door and Ezra heard it lock.

By feeling around he determined that the room, whatever its original purpose, was not more than eight feet square and nearly airtight. It was cold and damp, but they brought him four blankets and he lay down, more comfortable than he had been for many a night. So comfortable that in spite of all that had happened he was soon asleep.

Some time later he was wide awake, for the door was opening stealthily.

Chapter 18

"EASY, bub." Fess' whisper would not have disturbed a mouse.

Ezra slid out of his blankets where he was just getting warm and reached for Fess in the dark. They collided, he felt Fess' breath on his cheek and caught the words, "Let ourselves down the rope she's tied to the bank with. Swim to the big ship downstream. There's a boat tied under her stern. Cross the river in it."

They tiptoed through the open door to the deck. There was a splash of light at the far end of the barge, as though it came up the stairs from a cabin where the guards were probably warming themselves. How Fess knew the way didn't matter, he did know it and, without a wasted step, found the cable and went over the side. Ezra followed hand over hand, curling his feet up, for he dreaded the feel of that cold water. But it had to be done, so when he was clear of the barge he straightened his legs and was instantly soaked to his knees. He drew a deep breath and let go of the rope.

He sank without a sound and came up prickling all over and fighting the natural impulse to gasp aloud. As earlier in the evening, he found the water warmer than the air, but, mister, he would be cold when he got out of it! Fess had said a big ship downstream. That must be her rear lantern, or whatever they called the light on the end that was opposite the end hitched to the shore. There was no sign of life aboard. Probably the captain felt so safe in the midst of the army that guard duty was not strictly enforced. Still, you never could tell and it wouldn't pay to take chances. Ezra half swam and half floated to the side of the ship and felt his way along it. The rowboat was there and so was Fess, waiting to give him a hand over the side. How that man could get around night or day on land or in the water! And all the while talking like a deserter—the old fox!

Ezra climbed into the boat and the freezing air hit him. He crouched on his hands and knees, his mouth wide open to keep his teeth from rattling and his breath from whistling between his lips. The boat began to move and he heard the faint creak of oarlocks. The next sound would be a challenge, if the Yanks were on the job. He tried to have an answer ready, but his mind could think of nothing but the cold. He had never considered the James to be a large river until now, when it seemed miles wide. His hands were freezing and he dared not beat them, nor was there a second pair of oars to use. Nothing to do but huddle there while the wind stiffened his soaked clothing and the muscles beneath.

Finally, after what seemed hours, the boat slid into a mudbank and stopped. Fess stepped over the side and Ezra followed, concentrating on the problem of making no noise. The mud helped, for there was no gravel to crunch under foot; then, after a few steps, they were on frozen ground. The clouds lifted as they picked their way up the bank and approached what appeared to be a road. As they stepped down into it Ezra's numb feet caught on a root and he fell with a crash he fancied could be heard in Richmond.

"Who goes there!" A voice barked close by.

"Friend," he answered intuitively.

"Advance and give the countersign." There was a click as the sentry cocked his weapon.

While getting to his feet Ezra wondered if he and Fess could handle the armed man now that he was on guard. There would be at least one shot, enough to alert all the Yanks in the vicinity. He had an idea and answered in a thick voice, "Forgot countershine. Nezzer mind."

"Who are you?"

"Two gen'men—Company A—Gen'l Grant's army f'm Texas."

"You're drunk, you fool." The sentry's voice moderated.

"No, shur. Ain' drunk. Don' drink. Ain' had nushin' but water. Lishen!" He slapped his soaked clothing. "Jus' water."

"Blazes, boy!" The sentry stepped up and felt Ezra over. "You tumbled into the river. I should turn you in, but I won't. Get back to camp before you freeze to death."

"Yesh, shur. Come 'long, Mike."

"Is the other one drunk, too?" The sentry went over and felt of Fess, who said nothing but just stood their hiccough-ing and shaking. "Wet as a drownded rat! Move on, you idiots, don't stand there!"

They staggered across the road, through a field and stopped in a clump of trees.

"Good head work, bub," Fess whispered.

"I have a good teacher," Ezra answered. "For a while tonight I really thought you were a turncoat. Forgive me?"

"Shore. I had to fox the numskulls so they wouldn't put a guard over me."

"I see now."

"Overheard 'em talkin'. This outfit is Warren's Corps. Fixin' to move. We've got to get home 'n' tell the gen'ral."

"I'm almost froze, Fess. I mean it."

"Yeh, it hain't jest the kind of a night a feller'd pick to sleep in the barnyard with the gate open. Let's travel."

They skirted camps and dodged pickets for perhaps another hour, while their clothes froze stiff and cracked at every step. Dawn was not far away when something loomed up on a back road. They scouted it and identified it as a quartermaster's wagon abandoned because of a broken axle. Ezra stood guard while Fess investigated its load.

"Judas priest!" he said cautiously. "It's clo'es 'n' uniforms— ever'thing from caps to boots."

"Bless Abe Lincoln for getting 'em to us on time!"

As daylight broke, two Federal troopers in new uniforms walked briskly into a cavalry camp, saddled a couple of horses and rode away unchallenged. The older one, who was bow-legged and had huge hairy ears, took a chew of tobacco and remarked that polite people helped themselves and didn't bother folks.

"Fess," Ezra said, "I have been thinking."

"That's mebbe possible."

"Listen to me. Here we are right in the midst of Warren's Corps, that is getting ready to move somewhere. Why don't one of us find out the size of the force and where it's going before we report to the general? We'll pass as Yanks if we keep moving and don't say much."

"One of us?" Fess rolled an eye at him.

"Yes. You go tell the general what we already know. Then, as soon as I can, I'll come in with the rest of it."

"I s'pose you know what happens to a spy that gits ketched."

"I won't get caught."

"Not iffen I can help it you won't. We'll go 'long together 'n' call on Mr. Warren's boys."

"You make me mad, acting as though I can't take care of myself! Sometimes I'm tempted to beat you up."

"I know it." Fess nodded gravely. "That's why I keep a dog."

All that day they mixed with the Union troops without causing suspicion. They stayed in no one place for long, but they kept their eyes and ears open and learned what they wanted to know. Warren was moving his own corps, the Fifth, a division of the neighboring Second, a division of cavalry led by the often-met Gregg, and five batteries of field guns—nearly thirty-five thousand men all told. Exactly where they were going was a top secret, but they were heading south of Petersburg, probably to hit the Petersburg and Weldon railroad, one of the main supply lines for Lee's army.

"Nice fellers, them Yanks," Fess said as they rode away in the cold twilight. "Treated us like kinfolk, give us nice grub 'n' clo'es 'n' hosses. Ever see such a warm-hearted army, bub?"

"I never saw an army so well fed and equipped," Ezra answered gloomily. "They'll wear us out, Fess."

"Reckon so."

"Then why do we keep fighting?"

"Why does the north wind keep blowin'? Nature. Wind blows, water runs, men fight—nature."

"But men have intelligence."

"I wonder 'bout that." Fess led the way at a canter.

They passed through the lines easily and reported to Hampton, whose headquarters was a one-room cabin. He had been sitting at a table writing, and he leaned back to listen to them. His big frame was as sturdy-looking as the logs behind him, but his face showed thin through his beard and his eyes were tired.

"I can make you captains for this," was his first comment on their story. "How about it, Ezra?"

"It would be an honor, sir, but would there be any advantage?"

"In pay? No, for none of us get any pay. In work? Probably not. But," he glanced at a letter before him, "if I am transferred to some other field of operations, it would be easier to include you if you were an officer."

"Very well, sir."

"And you, Fess?"

"Suit yourself, Gen'ral." Fess shrugged. "But up in Cashier's Valley the fish won't bite no better for Cap'n Festival Jones'n for Private Jones."

"Those days in the valley, Fess!"

"There'll be more of 'em, Gen'ral."

"Will there be?" Hampton's big hands came together on

the table in such a grip that the frayed threads on his coat sleeves trembled. Then he relaxed suddenly. "Get some sleep," he said. "We may be afoot tomorrow."

They were. Lee acted quickly to protect the railroad and pulled Hill's Corps out of the Vicksburg trenches to save it. Half the men were barefooted and left bloody tracks on the snowy roads, but any kind of action was better to them than slowly freezing in those ditches. A brush with Federals might mean food, something to eat without gagging. Or it might mean shoes, even a pair of pants or an overcoat. The Yanks were good fellows when they offered such things for the price of a mere fight.

Hampton gathered what troopers he could and passed the infantry which, for all their misery, swung along like the veterans they were.

"Kid-glove soldiers!" they yelled at the cavalrymen. "Can't walk. Have to be toted wherever you go."

"Walking soldiers!" the riders jeered. "Couldn't ride a jack-ass. Cowtail regiment—always behind. Get there when the fighting stops and the eating starts."

With his few men Hampton could only hope to harry Warren's force, although he was master of that kind of skirmishing. First, however, he must overtake the Yanks, who had a long start. Once it would have been easy and pleasant, galloping through the country, shouting impolite remarks at the scared civilians, laughing, singing, with never a worry about the outcome. It was different now; horses and men were worn down before starting, there was no frisking, a short trot was an effort and a steady walk hard to maintain. Some still sang, but there were no rousing choruses, no mocking encores mixed with uncomplimentary repartee. The old gaiety was gone.

It proved to be the worst night Hampton and his men had ever known. With the darkness came a driving sleet that soaked them to the bone and then froze. Bridle reins stiffened like iron rods and numb, blue hands fumbled awkwardly to keep the ill-shod horses on the slippery roads. Those indefatigable officers rode up and down, slapping men who slumped in their saddles, cursing them until they roused, ordering them on.

Thanks to their new Federal outfits Ezra and Fess were in less distress. They were wet and miserable, but at least there were layers of cloth between their flesh and the ice, and the metal stirrups did not burn their bare toes. Also they had had several good meals recently, even hot coffee in the Yankee camps. That was something to remember and dream about on such a night.

"If you think this is cold you should have seen me in the middle of the James River night before last," Ezra said to the man beside him, thinking that conversation might help keep the fellow awake.

The trooper did not answer. Ez leaned over and touched his leg, then shook him. Without a sound the man pitched sideways and fell against him, a dead weight. Ezra held him up and stopped the column.

"What's wrong there?" an officer asked, a few ranks behind.

"Man fainted, sir," Ezra answered.

He felt for the trooper's heart and found he was wearing no shirt, only a ragged jacket held together with strings.

"Anybody got a drink of liquor for him?" the officer called out, riding up on the other side.

"Sure," a bitter voice mocked, "plenty of liquor and roast turkey, a big fire and a feather bed. We always have such things, we do."

A few men laughed. Others began swearing at the delay, for a pause made them feel colder.

"He won't need anything, sir," Ezra said. "He's dead."

"Oh, well." The officer sounded relieved. "I'll help you lay him beside the road."

They rode on, the dead man's horse keeping in line from habit. They were on the right track, for farmers whom they routed out of bed said a Union army had passed that way the day before. The riders hunched their shoulders and bent in strange positions, trying to rub freezing spots and warm their fingers with their horses' breath. During the night four more men froze to death.

It was noon and still storming when they caught up with Warren at Hicksford. He had already torn up miles of railroad tracks and was still busy at it, but his pursuers had too little life left to attack. They camped at a distance and managed to put up such a bold front that the Federals never guessed how exhausted they were. Where they found food, even a little of it, for themselves and their horses and where they got fuel for the fires that thawed them out, no man could say, for each did his own foraging. But they did find it, and within twenty-four hours were in their saddles again. By then the infantry and artillery, after an equally heroic march, had joined them and moved against the enemy. Even Hampton, who had come to expect miracles from his men, was astounded at their resilience.

It was not a hot fight, for the Federals, too, were cold and tired. They had carried out their mission of destruction and, not knowing their opponents' strength, thought it wise to retire. The Southern infantry stayed behind to round up Negroes and repair the railroad, but Hampton was on the Yankees' heels, jabbing, snapping, driving them to cover, as his dogs so often had driven bears in the days before he turned to hunting men.

This time he was not in at the kill, for another sleet storm swept down from the north with such fury that even he dared not face it. Slowly, walking and leading his horse much of the way to keep from freezing, he led his men back to the old camping ground near Petersburg. He had saved the railroad and postponed the fall of Richmond for a little while, but he finally knew that the once mighty Army of Northern Virginia was on its last legs and the end of the war not far off.

They lay in camp through that awful November and December. One evening toward the middle of January, 1865, the general stopped on a round of the quarters. He entered the shack where Ezra and Fess were frying mule meat in a saucepan they had hammered out of a canteen.

"Good evening, fellow officers." He half smiled.

"Good evening, sir!" Ezra was the first on his feet. "Does that mean we are commissioned?"

"Yes, the papers came through today."

"We're obleeged, Gen'ral." Fess stood up and spoke without enthusiasm.

Hampton looked at the frying meat and turned away.

"We are leaving here tomorrow," he said. "General Lee is sending me to rally South Carolina against Sherman."

"We are leaving General Lee, sir!"

"Yes, Ezra. So is Hoke's Division, Connor's Brigade, Butler's Division—going back for a last—to make a stand at home. Good evening, gentlemen." He turned sharply and went out.

"It has come," Ezra said unhappily.

"Yeh." Fess stooped and stroked an imaginary head. "Come on, Spot, we're goin' home."

Chapter 19

THE decision to send Hampton home to defend Columbia was largely of sentimental value. In the Carolinas there were fragments of horse and foot which, if they could have been assembled in one place, might have provided a force of twenty-five thousand men. But they were scattered, transportation had broken down, and the cavalry units were almost useless as such because of the lack of horses. The best the general could do at the moment was to gather less than three thousand troopers to oppose Sherman's victorious army, now swinging north. The capital of South Carolina had no fortifications or natural defenses of any kind so Hampton decided not to defend the city, thus giving the Federal commander no legitimate excuse for harming it.

Ezra had not been home since he left ahead of the sheriff four years before. He remembered it as a boy and now wanted to see it with a man's eyes, so one afternoon he got leave for a few hours and rode back along the familiar road. It was almost warm, although February was only half gone, and the sun cheered him. Little else did, for the face of the land had an unhappy, uncared-for look. Most white workers had been in the army for years and the Negroes had run away to join their supposed liberators, who had nothing more substantial to give them than high-sounding promises. Neglect was everywhere; weeds, broken fences, buildings in disrepair,

fallow fields and ragged people summed up the years of shortages and deprivations.

Still, for that afternoon Ezra felt the peace that always
comes when nature is undisturbed by man. When he saw
the gate leading to the *Sand Hills* pasture he was tempted to
go in and over the hill to the place where Fess had taught him
to ride. That was sure a long while ago! Long in years and
long in experience it seemed to him. That is the way with
time, flowing along, sometimes for generations with no par-
ticular excitement, then the current quickens and during
mere months men and nations are swept to destinations of
which they never dreamed.

When he came in sight of the *Sand Hills* mansion he was
not surprised by its empty look. He knew Mrs. Hampton and
the younger children had left and the slaves had joined the
aimless exodus of their people. Only one person was in sight,
a Negro scratching with a rake in one of the flower beds at
the lower end of the lawn.

"Hi, Jeems!" Ezra stopped his horse as he recognized the
house boy. "How have you been since I went away?"

" 'Skuse me, suh." Jeems straightened up. "Ah disregards
meetin' yo'."

"Don't you remember the boy from down the creek who
mended a leg here after a bear fight four years ago?"

"Oh me, oh my!" Jeems' face was suddenly all eyes and
teeth. "Iffen hit hain't Mistah Ezra all 'live 'n' growed up!"

"Sure is. How are you, Jeems?"

"Ah hain't happy, suh."

"How does it happen you're still here?"

"Yo' t'ink Ah's one ob dem trash niggers dat run off cayse de do' am open? Huh! Missy say, 'Ah s'pose, Jeems, yo' go too.' Ah say, 'Go whar? Chase atter de Yankees dat kills Marse Presson 'n' Marse Frank? No, ma'm! Ah stays whar Ah is wid my own folkses.' "

"Good boy! That pleased Mrs. Hampton."

"She cry, suh."

"There's plenty to cry about, Jeems."

"Yas, suh. De Yankees mak' one heap o' trouble. Ol' Satan hisse'f mus' wear a blue coat 'n' shoot off his mouf 'bout ever'-body gwine be happy cayse a wah mak' ever'body mizzable. Yo' git yo'se'f a Yankee, suh?"

"Yes, I got a few, I s'pose."

"Hallylulyer! Come up to de big house 'n' have some vittles 'n' drink."

"Any of the family home?"

"Jes' me, suh. Nobody else on de place."

"I must be getting along." Ezra flicked his horse. "Take care of things, Jeems."

"Yas, suh."

Ezra rode down the road, curious to see if Jed Sears' shack was still standing. Not that the sight of it would stir pleasant memories, but it had been his home and he had a natural wish to visit it again, especially as he had been told Jed had left some time ago. It was there, though brush nearly hid it now. He rode up to the door, recalling the day he had seen the step littered with the torn pages of his precious *Ivanhoe*. A book more or less was a small thing in this upset world, but the thought of it made him angry.

"Wal, mister?"

The well-known voice was behind him and he wheeled his horse to face Jed. The man looked about the same, dirty, drooping yellow mustache, shifty pale-blue eyes and, as usual, he leaned against something, this time a small tree.

"Well!" Ezra gave him a long look. "I thought you weren't here."

"Ez!" Jed's mouth dropped open.

"Going to call the sheriff this time?"

"No! Bygones is bygones, Ez." Jed took a step forward, his hand held out.

"That's the proper spirit, but I don't believe you feel that way," Ezra said evenly. "No, I don't want to shake hands with you."

"Now, boy, that hain't no kind of talk to give me. I allus thought a heap uv you. I've missed you turrible."

"When there was work to do."

"Now, Ez, you—Jeez!" Jed's eyes opened almost wide. "Them things on yore shoulder says you're a cap'n. You done well in the army. Must git big pay."

"Oh, yes, all officers are rich."

"I knowed you'd do well with our good neighbor Hampton to help you along. We're mighty proud uv Ginr'l Hampton."

"Oh, shut up, Jed," Ezra said wearily. "You hate the general and you hate me same as you did. Why lie about it?"

"Still talk right out like you used to. Did when you was a boy. That reminds me, Bert's in the North army. His conscience just wouldn't let him go nowheres else."

"I know all about Bert," Ezra snapped. "He joined the

North so he could get more pay and he's been robbing the
dead and wounded ever since. I've got enough on him to hang
him, if I ever get my hands on him."

"I jest can't hear you talk so, Ez." Jed pushed himself away
from the tree and stood alone. "I'm goin' in the house."

"Not right now you ain't." Ezra touched a pistol at his belt.
"Walk straight ahead of me to the road."

"What you mean?" Jed's eyes narrowed.

"I'm not giving you a chance to shoot me in the back."

"Now, Ez, you don't mean that."

"I do. You're no different than you ever were, Jed. You or
Bert would shoot me without turning a hair if you got the
chance. March!"

When they reached the highway Ezra rode away without
another word. Had he glanced back he would have seen a
look on Jed's face that would have shamed a rattlesnake.

The next morning, February seventeenth, Sherman's army
was in sight. Behind it a trail of blood and ashes stretched
back to Savannah and Atlanta. It was not an expedition
against mere military objectives, but the most ruthless piece of
destruction so far known in civilized warfare. Undefended
cities, villages and private dwellings had been looted and
burned and the country, down to the last ear of corn and the
last hen's egg, had been pillaged. Much of it was pure van-
dalism, condoned if not encouraged by the man whose only
excuse was the expression he coined: War is hell.

The South was shocked and furious, but too exhausted to
resist in force. Hampton had less than three thousand men

and those he withdrew from Columbia to eliminate any pretense Sherman might have for attacking the city. At the same
time the mayor went out to meet Sherman and explain the
situation, reminding him that the people were noncombatants
and entitled to consideration. That night Columbia was
burned. "Utterly ruined," the Union commander wrote
proudly in later years when recording the crime.

Across the river a handful of Confederate soldiers watched
the flames in impotent fury.

"Where is the general?" Ezra asked Fess, whom he found
cursing aloud at the sky.

"Dunno. Rode by here a spell ago stiff's a dead man."

"Do you suppose he has gone out to *Sand Hills* to try to
save a few things?"

"I told you, I dunno where he is. You don't reckon they'll
burn that too, do you?"

"Sure. They hate him."

"Iffen that's where he is, he'll need help. Come on, bub!"

They rode hard, thankful for something to do. *Sand Hills*
was dark as they approached, but when they pulled up at the
door it opened and Jeems stood there, a lantern in one hand
and a butcher knife in the other.

"We hain't harborin' no strangers," he said with enormous
dignity. "No suh! De house am full ob folkses ternight."

"All right, Jeems," Ezra sang out. "This is Ezra Todd and
a friend."

"Oh me, oh my!" Relief filled the boy's voice. "Praise de
Lawd 'n' bless de angels, suh!"

"Is General Hampton here?"

"No, suh, nobody hain't hyah 'ceptin' me. But we got plenty food. Yo' genmens come in 'n' set yo'se'fs ter eat."

"Sounds good, eh, Fess?"

" 'Twouldn't be polite to say no. Good manners're more important than pusnal wishes."

They hitched their horses at the back of the house and entered the kitchen, where Jeems was already slinging food with both hands. There was plenty of it, as he had said, even when they finished. They made little conversation in the room that was partly lighted by the burning city two miles away.

"Yo' speck de debbils come hyar, suh?" Jeems finally asked.

"Not tonight. They're too busy looting."

"Mebbe Marse Wade fotch his sojers hyar tomorrer."

"That is possible."

"Why don't we stay?" Fess spoke up. "We might be's useful here's anywheres."

Ezra agreed to that, so by turns they stood watch through the night. Nothing happened. Before dawn the wind changed so that daylight found the country wrapped in heavy smoke from the city. For that reason they did not see the Federal horsemen until they galloped into the yard.

"Quick, Jeems! Bring us all the firearms and ammunition you can find." Ezra drew his pistol. "You take the back of the house, Fess, I'll take the front."

"Mistah Ezra!" Jeems's eyes rolled with terror. "Missy done took away ever' gun so de Yankees couldn't 'skuse demse'fs fo' burnin' de house."

"Hey!" Ezra stopped in the middle of the floor. "Why didn't we think of that, Fess? If we defend the place they'll surely burn it."

"Reckon so," Fess said calmly. He looked through a back window. "We can't git away, we're surrounded."

"If we fight, the general will lose his house. We can't let that happen—not if the Yanks will spare it and treat us as prisoners of war."

"Yeh! What's a Yank promise worth?"

"We've got to risk it, Fess. We've no right to turn this house into a fort and let the Hamptons lose their home. What do you say?"

"We'll quit," Fess answered.

Ezra caught up a napkin from the table and ran down the hall to the front door, which he opened enough to wave the flag of truce.

"Come out!" someone yelled.

Ezra pulled the door wide open and stepped out with Fess beside him. Below on the lawn were perhaps twenty Union cavalrymen, red-eyed, disheveled, and dangerously drunk. An irregular line of pickets stretched out of sight around each side of the house.

"I want to speak with the officer in command," Ezra shouted.

"Sherman or Grant?" A soldier answered and all roared.

"Either one, I'm not fussy."

"What you want, Reb?" A captain, or a man in a captain's uniform, walked up to the foot of the steps, a pistol in each hand.

"We will surrender if you will treat us as prisoners of war and respect this house as private property. What do you say?"

"Sure, sure." The officer was weaving on his feet.

"Drunk's a fool," Fess muttered. "But they've got us." He walked down the steps and Ezra followed.

"We give our word not to escape," Ezra said.

"We know Johnnies." The captain waved his pistols carelessly. "Tie 'em up, boys."

" 'N' we know Yanks," Fess said, as four men began tying their arms behind them.

"Like 'em?" The captain grinned foolishly.

"Love 'em. Sweetest meat I ever et. Fry 'em in axle grease 'n' you don't notice that natchel dirty taste."

"That's an inshult to the United Shtates of America!" The captain shouted.

"Shut up, Bill, you're drunk. I'll handle this now."

Ezra twisted around and faced Bert Sears. The big fellow was leering in the old open-mouthed manner and, strangely enough, he was cold sober.

"We hain't met up fer quite a spell, Ez," he jeered.

"I'm surprised you're still unhanged," Ezra retorted.

"There's more s'prises comin' to you," Bert promised.

"Now shee here," the captain put in. "I'm a offisher and I give thish Reb my word."

"Yeh," Bert sneered, "I know how you come to be a officer— don't fergit that. What's more you gived me yore word I could run things this time."

"We didn't know theshe Johnnies wash here then."

"That's our good luck. Here"—Bert pulled a bottle of whisky from his pocket—"take this 'n' git out."

The captain clutched the bottle and wobbled away.

"Nice army the Yanks got," Fess remarked.

"We're fiddlin' now 'n' you fellers'll dance." Bert pulled a pistol. "Foller me up them steps. You fellers," to the soldiers, "come 'long behind." For some reason they were willing to take orders from him.

"And if we don't?" Ezra asked.

"You will." Bert started up the steps, then turned, and shouted, "Pa! Pa, come hyar."

Jed Sears shuffled around the corner of the house.

"Jeez!" He brought his sagging lower jaw up. "Ez—'n' all tied up tight, too."

"When did you enlist?" Ezra snapped.

"I didn't." Jed shook his head. "I jest come over to see the fun."

Bert led the way into the house and the prisoners followed, for they were helpless to do otherwise. Bert tramped down the hall to one of the parlors, the one where governors and scholars had so often been entertained, and stood a few feet inside the door looking around. His face was flushed and his small eyes flickered like a snake's tongue.

"I been waitin' years to git in hyar," he said slowly. "I wasn't good 'nough to mix with the Hamptons like you was, Ez. Quality folkses didn't see me. Yeh, I been waitin' years fer this."

He emptied his revolver into a beautiful mirror that reached from floor to ceiling.

"Cut loose, boys!" he yelled to the soldiers. "Help yoreselfs, but don't start no fire." The men whooped and scattered.

"What do you think you are doing!" Ezra cried.

Bert slammed the door and backed against it.

"I'm doin' just what I allus wanted to do." He was panting with excitement. "I hate the Hamptons, ever' damn one of 'em. I hate you, Ez, that's why I fotched you hyar to watch." He shot down a crystal chandelier.

Ezra glanced at Fess who was white with fury.

"Pa hates 'em too," Bert went on, in a mockingly confidential tone. "Hain't the ol' man enjoyin' hisself though!"

Jed had pulled out his sheath knife and was ripping the tapestry off chairs and sofas. Then he picked up a bronze lamp and crashed it down on a mahogany table.

"Yeh"—Bert watched his father proudly—"hit does me good to see him so happy."

"What'd you say your pappy's name is?" Fess asked blandly.

"Sears."

"Oh. I thought mebbe it was Sherman."

"That's a good un!" Bert laughed loudly. "I sorta like you, mister. You don't look like quality folkses."

"You can't tell by the looks of a toad how fer he can hop," Fess said. "My pappy was Napoleon Bonyparte and my mammy was the Queen of Sheby."

"I believe you would joke with the devil," Ezra said in an angry aside.

"That's what I'm doin'," Fess answered.

When the room had been wrecked, Bert opened the door

and motioned them across the hall into the library. From all parts of the house came sounds of tearing and smashing, running feet and loud voices. A soldier was coming down the stairs with his arms full of shawls. His spurs caught on a tread and he rolled to the bottom, while someone leaned over the banister and pelted him with china teacups. Bert roared with laughter, for things were going better than he had hoped.

"You like books, Ez," he said genially. " 'Member the one you fotched home from hyar. All puffed up you was 'cause the great Wade Hampton gived hit to you. Look at all these purty books! Mighty valuable, hain't they? Wuth thousands uv dollars. Eddycated gen'men like you 'n' Wade Hampton'd feel awful bad iffen anything happened to 'em, wouldn't you?"

"Yes," Ezra agreed and instantly wished he had not said it.

Bert closed the door and pushed a table against it, then took down a leather-bound volume and slashed its covers with his knife. He tore out a handful of pages, threw the book through a window, and attacked more books, working faster and faster like a madman.

"Better not, bub," Fess said quietly, as Ezra struggled with his ropes. "The more you tug at the knots the tighter they git."

Ezra stood panting and looking around. He was glad to see that the family portraits had been removed, along with the silver candlesticks. Perhaps Mrs. Hampton had had time to get away with all the valuables. Bert finally stopped slashing at the books, realizing he could not cut up ten thousand of them. Jed found a gold-headed cane and walked around knocking figurines and bric-a-brac from the tops of bookcases. A marble bust of George Washington would not shatter so he took it in both hands and hurled it into a fireplace.

Bert drove his prisoners through the lower rooms for some time after that, forcing them to watch the destruction. The soldiers were mainly interested in loot and in their mad search for it had smashed furniture, ripped off paneling, and even torn up some of the floors. It was according to plan so far, but they had found liquor and would get out of hand sooner or later.

Bert led the way upstairs followed by Ezra and Fess who were forced along by Jed with a cocked pistol. They entered one of the bedrooms and Bert closed and locked the door.

"You're tired, Ez," he said with mock sympathy. "Jest you lay down on the bed 'n' rest."

"What are you up to now?" Ezra glared at him.

"You wouldn't argy with me, Ez."

Ezra considered. With their hands bound, he and Fess could fight only with their feet against these two armed men. It would be foolhardy to try it. Their only chance was to go along and hope for a break.

"No, I won't argue with you," he said, laying himself on the bed.

Bert took a roll of cord from his pocket and lashed Ezra's ankles to the bedposts, whistling a tune between his teeth as he worked. Jed stood behind Fess, itching for an excuse to shoot.

"Now, Ez, I'm goin' to say good-by." Bert stepped back and looked down at him, an evil smile on his beefy face. "I been waitin' a long while to say jest that to you." He turned to his father. "Take yore man out, Pa."

"Stiddy, bub," Fess said in a desperately quiet voice. "We'll finish this job later."

"Heads up, Fess," Ezra answered.

Jed put a pistol between Fess' shoulder blades and forced him into the hall. Bert followed and slammed the door.

Ezra lay there, wet with the sweat of helplessness. If Bert had blustered and threatened it would have been understandable, but his air of mocking friendliness was puzzling. For long minutes Ezra struggled furiously with his bonds, but it was no use. Finally he lay still, trying to guess Bert's next move.

Suddenly it was sickeningly clear; he caught a faint smell of smoke and heard fire crackling downstairs.

Chapter 20

THEY forced Fess downstairs, took a picket rope from a saddle and tied him to a tree on the lawn facing the house. Soldiers were everywhere, sprawling on the ground, sitting on horses, leaning against each other, all drunk and waiting for something. Their loot was small, no money, jewelry or silver, and they were sullen. Bert and Jed re-entered the house and closed the door. A few minutes later they opened it wide and stepped out. Behind them in the hall a fire of broken furniture was blazing and smoke was pouring up the staircase.

"My Gawd!" Fess shouted. "There's a man in there! He'll burn alive!"

Some of the soldiers started toward the steps, but Bert waved them back.

"Thar's a Johnny in thar," he told them, "but he's dead."

"Sure?" a man asked.

"Yeh. Hain't he, Pa?"

Jed hesitated, for he lacked his son's experience as a killer. Then he caught Bert's eye. "Shore. I—I reckon he is."

"They're lyin'!" Fess struggled frantically. "They're burnin' him. He's tied to a bed. They're burnin' him alive!"

"He wuz alive." Bert grinned.

"Yanks!" Fess' voice rose shrilly. "Git him out. He's upstairs."

"The stairs are blazing to the top," a Federal pointed out.

"They wouldn't do that anyway. They're pulling your leg, Reb."

"Cut me loose!" Fess screamed. "I'll go. Cut me loose!"

"You're smart, but you don't fool us," Bert growled.

"Captain!" Fess caught sight of the befuddled officer. "You won't let 'em do it! The boy's helpless in there!"

"Housh afire?" The captain blinked.

"Gawd, man, wake up! Cut me loose if you're a Christian." Froth flew from Fess' lips. "I'll come back."

"Shur." The captain staggered toward him. "We don't burn people. Ain't Injuns." He fumbled with his sword.

Without a word Bert stepped up and knocked him down. Some of the men laughed.

"Been a private I'd'a shot him—tryin' to free a prisoner." Bert glared at the soldiers. "I'm boss hyar. Drink yer rum 'n' mind yer business." He pulled a revolver and they backed off, the officer crawling after them.

For the first time in his life Festival Jones fainted. When he came to the mansion of *Sand Hills* was blazing to the sky.

The soldiers lay about the place all day in the sunshine sleeping off their liquor. Fess was left bound to the tree and no one offered him food or drink. Bert and Jed were the only sober ones, as they wanted all their senses for the enjoyment of their triumph. It was a great day for them and they walker up and down, gloating over the ruins and recalling the time the Hampton family had refused to treat them as equals. An they abused Ezra with every vile word they knew for his friendship with the Hamptons.

Fess listened without saying a word. A deeper anger than

he had ever known was in his heart, but his head was clear. If there was any justice on earth he would somehow bring it to bear on those brutes, but first he must get out of their power. They had committed hideous crimes against the two people he loved most, yet he must act indifferent. Once such a lack of emotion would have excited suspicion, but war had hardened men until brutality was expected. So with outward calm he stared at the smoking ashes in silence.

When evening came Bert mounted his captive on a horse and they rode back toward Columbia. A soldier with a prisoner was nothing new so they passed unchallenged around the smouldering city and out to the picket lines which were loosely held at that place.

Bert stopped the horses in a clump of trees and ordered, "Git down."

"Yes, sir." Fess' voice was almost pleasant. He slid to the ground.

"You're free now."

"Then cut my hands loose."

"No, you might pitch inter me 'n' I'd have to shoot you. I don't want to do that 'cause I want you to git safe back to ol' Wade Hampton 'n' tell him all you've seed today. Don't skip none of it."

"I won't," Fess promised.

"Wish I could be thar to see him squirm." Bert chuckled. "Be shore to tell him hit wuz Bert Sears that done hit. Don't fergit to tell him that."

"I won't," Fess repeated.

"Now git!" Bert turned the horses and disappeared.

Fess walked until he found a Confederate who freed his hands.

"Been tied up long?" the soldier asked.

"All day."

"But you finally fooled 'em, eh?"

"Yeh. Know where Gen'ral Hampton is?"

"Down the road, first barn you come to."

"Much obleeged." Fess walked on, swinging his numb hands.

He found Hampton with his staff, sitting on crates around an overturned wagon box and examining maps by the light of a lantern. He waited until the officers left, then knocked and entered when bidden.

"Fess!" Hampton turned. "I wondered where you were all day."

"Wish to Gawd I didn't have to tell you, Gen'ral." Tears rolled down the rough cheeks.

"What is it, Fess?"

Slowly, in a tired voice, Fess told the story. Hampton took it without flinching, but his great fists tightened and the veins in his neck twisted.

"The poor boy! The poor boy! Only a few miles away and I could not raise a finger to help him!"

"Nor me." Fess stared into the darkness beyond the lantern. "I was only a few rods away."

"By heaven!" Hampton drove a fist into the other palm. "By heaven, Fess, this score shall be settled!"

"You can't fetch back the boy or the house, Gen'ral."

"The house was nothing; it was written off long ago. The

North hates South Carolina most of all the states and me most of all Carolinians. I knew Sherman would destroy my property."

"Even Sherman wouldn't have—have burned the boy, Gen'ral."

"Certainly not. It was the Searses who did that. Especially Bert who leads a gang of his own stamp."

"The Yanks was too drunk to realize what was goin' on," Fess said fairly. "They wouldn't have allowed it iffen they'd knowed."

"To be weak at such a time!" Hampton began walking up and down. "I can't even return to *Sand Hills* and bury the boy's ashes. Once we could have cut our way through, but now—" He stretched his arms in a wide gesture. "*Quintilius varus*—give me back my legions!*"

"Eh?" Fess stared at him.

"A Roman emperor said that, and his heart was not as full as mine, I do believe."

"Yeh, yeh," was all Fess could say.

"Have you eaten today, Fess?" Hampton's voice was normal again.

"No, sir."

"Nor I, but we must. I have a ham and white bread Mrs. Hampton sent in by one of the servants. By the way, what became of Jeems?"

"Last I see of him he was headin' downstairs scairt half to death."

"Poor Jeems. But the Yankees wouldn't harm him. Come, Fess, eat. We have work to do."

Work, yes, heartbreaking work that offered no promise of success. After the fall of Columbia, General Johnston had drawn back toward the north, trying to collect the scattered Confederate forces in that section. Hampton, with not more than four thousand men, was his right hand with which he tried to hold Sherman while the reforming was in progress. Kilpatrick, whom the gray troopers had fought so often, was back in command of Sherman's cavalry spearheading the advance. The old enemies were face to face once more, but this time the tide was running strong for the north.

The Confederates were short of everything except spirit. It was not the former air of reckless gaiety, but a cold, grim determination to fight to the last ditch. News of the tragedy at *Sand Hills* had spread through the little command, creating a thirst for revenge that could only be quenched by action. They knew no enemy officer had instigated the crime, yet it blended so easily into the black record of Sherman's army that it became part of it. Fess kept to himself and said little, but the look on his face and the vicious way he sought combat betrayed his thoughts.

Hampton's sense of justice forbade his blaming the whole Federal army for what had happened, yet the incident crystallized the grimness that had been growing upon him. His kindness toward his men was as marked as ever, but his regard for the enemy was what, in a lesser man, would have been called hatred. The sight of a blue uniform made his jaw set and prisoners in his hands received not a whit more consideration than the laws of warfare decreed. This was a new Hampton, whose savage instincts were leashed by a powerful

hand. Even the death of Preston had not given him such
bitterness. That had been the fortune of war suffered on a
fair field; this was a betrayal of all decency by neighbors whom
he had never wronged. Like the men under him, he could
not quite disassociate it from the Union army. His longing to
hit back was deep and furious and, when Sherman threatened
to execute a Confederate prisoner for every Federal shot for
pillaging, he roared back the answer: "For every soldier of
mine murdered by you, I shall have executed at once two of
yours, giving in all cases preference to any officers who may
be in my hands." Sherman did not carry out the threat.

Screening Johnston's movements as best he could and re-
treating before crushing numbers, Hampton fought a battle
at Kellytown on the twenty-fourth of February. Two weeks
later on a rainy night near the North Carolina line, he picked
up a Yankee patrol and learned that Kilpatrick's whole force
was bivouacked a few miles away. With all the cunning of
the old raiding days the gray riders crept up to the sleeping
camp and charged. At first it was a wild stampede. Kilpatrick
himself escaped clad only in underwear and slippers, but he
rallied his men and they fought back furiously. That was the
difference from the early war years; the Yanks were soldiers
now, as good as any. Hampton could not carry through against
such numbers, but he got away with five hundred captives
and one hundred and fifty released Confederate prisoners.

"Nice little fight," Fess muttered to himself. "You'd 'ave
liked it, bub."

Hampton took instant advantage of Kilpatrick's upset to
ride around him and seize the road to Fayetteville, where

Johnston's troops were crossing the river. But the Federals followed faster than he thought, and as he ate breakfast alone in a hotel he heard shots in the street. When he got into the saddle the commander of all the Southern cavalry had only five men to command. Coming up the street was a troop of more than sixty Yankee horsemen.

The brooding, gloomy Hampton of recent days was replaced in a flash by the old fire-eater.

"With me, boys!" he thundered. "Charge!"

And they did charge. It was not like Brandy Station or Gettysburg, it was more glorious. All the fury and valor of an army was packed into those six men as they galloped into the midst of ten times their number. The sound of their meeting brought people into the street, then the whistle of bullets sent them back. The Yankees' horses reared as Hampton's big charger, fighting with hoofs and teeth, knocked them right and left. The general emptied two saddles with his pistol and two more with his sword. The five men beside him were almost as good. The Federals dropped back toward the river and disappeared around a corner.

"They're coming behind us!" someone yelled and the six, miraculously unwounded, turned to face them again.

This time Hampton changed his tactics and ordered his troopers to sit still and pick them off. The bluecoats opened up with carbines and came on, but they must have been poor shots for not a Confederate fell. They just sat there as calmly as though out for target practice and dropped the Northerners one by one. When thirteen lay in the street and others were wounded, the Federals broke and ran. The doughty six followed with such a whoop and burst of shots that the Yankee captain and a dozen of his men surrendered.

As he sheathed his sword, Hampton smiled for the first time in days and called out, "It seems like old times, Fess "

"Not to me," Fess answered and turned away quickly.

On the afternoon of that day Fess was riding alone beyond the river. He was often alone now. A cavalry patrol came up the road escorting two prisoners it had picked up. That had become routine of late, for Sherman's "bummers" were so eager to plunder that they neglected the usual precautions. Absently Fess reined aside to let them pass—then stiffened in his saddle.

"Halt!" His high-pitched voice roared.

"Yes, sir." The lieutenant in command saluted, then inquired casually, "What's up, Captain Jones?"

"It's them hellions!" Fess whipped out a pistol and poised it in a hand that trembled. Then he lowered it. "No, we don't do business that way. Lieutenant, hold 'em till I come back. Let 'em give you the slip 'n' I'll shoot every one of you." He galloped back up the road, his face white.

Bert Sears ran his tongue over his dry lips and said to the lieutenant, "You've got to help me, sir. That feller made a mistake. I hain't no Yank. It jest happens I'm wearin' a Yank uniform like most all Johnnies do."

The officer ignored him.

Jed leaned against a small roadside tree and whimpered, "I hain't no sojer. Cain't you see I hain't got no uniform on? I'm a honest farmer—Jim Butler's my name. I never hurted nobody. Please, mister, let me go so's I can git home to my wife 'n' pore little chillun."

The lieutenant ignored him also.

"Mister—sir—my father's a rich man in Charleston." Bert made a supreme effort to sound confident. "You let me loose 'n' I'll send ever'one of you fellers five thousan' dollars. Hain't that better'n lettin' a innocent man be murdered jest 'cause a stranger made a mistake? I've got the money 'n' I'll—"

"Shut up!" the lieutenant roared.

Hoofs clattered on the road and Fess and General Hampton came around a bend. The big man on the big horse may well have looked like the angel of death to the prisoners. He pulled up and gave them a long, steady look that made even the guards move uneasily.

"Gentlemen," he said, spacing his words carefully to control his voice, "these are the savages who burned Captain Todd alive. There is no question of their guilt, but they shall have a trial by court-martial. Lieutenant, conduct them to the crossroads."

"Yes, sir."

Within half an hour the military court convened under an oak tree by the roadside. A colonel on Hampton's staff presided and the proceedings were scrupulously legal. Not a word or a minute was wasted as the general looked on, grim and tight-lipped. Bert Sears, a Federal soldier, and his father, a civilian, were found guilty of the murder of Captain Ezra Todd, C.S.A. and sentenced to immediate execution by hanging.

"Gen'ral, we're ol' neighbors," Bert blubbered wildly. "Ez 'n' we wuz like brothers. You know I never done nothin' to harm him."

"I fotched him up same's my own boy." Jed held out his hands in a frantic gesture for mercy.

Hampton turned his back and walked toward his horse.

Jed reeled and Bert caught him in his arms; then, holding him as a shield, he wheeled toward the woods. Rifles cracked and Jed slumped on the grass. Bert lurched for the tree trunk as Festival Jones' pistol spoke once.

Fess walked over and looked at the dead men and the soldiers heard him say, "We've did what we could for you, Ez."

For days after that, the stubborn retreat continued beyond the Cape Fear River. Johnston's army now comprised the fragments of many commands, a scant twenty thousand hungry, ragged men who formed, in one respect, a comic-opera force, inasmuch as it included three generals, four lieutenant generals and twelve major generals. Close behind, Sherman's sixty thousand were sweeping the country clean.

Many of the Carolinians had seen their own homes destroyed and their bitterness was too great to be borne. They must strike back, no matter what the cost. Johnston appreciated their attitude and, on March seventeenth, asked Hampton to select a place for battle. The general chose Bentonville, because the surrounding country was wooded and had few roads the Federals could use. So they made a stand there.

For the last time Hampton played his old role of holding against tremendous odds while the infantry got into position.

As always, he did not fail. The outcome of the battle was inevitable, but the fact that the battered force of Confederate odds and ends fought for four days before Sherman's horde could gain a decision was a victory in itself. Still in character as he left the stage, Hampton led a charge that held the bridge, over which what was left of Johnston's army made its escape.

They continued to fall back, for how long and to where no one knew. They could not stop nor could they keep on much longer as they were. On April ninth came the word that Lee had surrendered to Grant. This was it, but still Hampton would not believe it. It was possible, he said, for the other armies to retire beyond the Mississippi and continue to fight in Texas or even seek sanctuary in Mexico. He, for one, was not ready to talk about surrender.

But Johnston was, for like Lee he realized that further resistance would bring unjustified suffering. On the thirteenth he sent a dispatch to Sherman asking for a conference. The Yankee general, now that he had won, ceased to be vindictive and ordered a truce. The talks dragged on for days, Hampton disapproving of the whole thing. With all his old vigor he wrote Jefferson Davis, who was fleeing south from Richmond, about his Texas plan and begged the president to go with him. *My men are in hand and will follow me anywhere*, he penned in a firm hand.

Davis approved of the plan and the two met at Charlotte, where the president authorized Hampton to arrange the proposed flight across the Mississippi. It was during that day that Johnston surrendered his army to Sherman. Hampton knew his command was gone forever. In one of the most touching scenes of his life he said good-by to his men and the troopers cried like children. But the general, personally, would not quit. He insisted that inasmuch as he and some of his staff had been absent, they were not included in the surrender terms. Resistance was out of the question, but they would find Davis and perhaps help him escape.

Wrapped in the gloom of defeat, each man reviewing those four lost years as he had seen them, Hampton and his faithful handful rode all day through the rain and deepening mud. At Charlotte they learned that Davis had fled, perhaps to Yorkville, South Carolina. No one was sure. Hampton was the only one of the party not exhausted—even Festival Jones was ready to give up. The general sent them to bed, then found himself a fresh horse and went on alone.

Fess tumbled into an empty horse stall in a livery stable and slept like the planks on which he lay until a boy shook him some time after daylight.

"Am yo' Gennel Hampton, sur?"

"Me?" Fess sat up. "No, I'm Methusaler, though I feel older."

"A officer jes' rid in say he got ter see Gennel Hampton."

"Find out where he is, boy, or I'll skin you alive," a voice shouted outside.

Fess rose cautiously, eyes wide and mouth open. Crouching like a cat, he tiptoed to the door and peeked out.

"Judas priest!" In one leap he was outside. "Bub!"

"You old sinner!" Ezra swung to the ground. "Where have you been?"

"Where've I been!" Fess gave him a bear hug. "Where've you been? We s'posed you was dead—burned up."

"Oh, no." Ezra laughed to see the old trooper so upset. "Jeems got me out. Cut me loose after Bert left. The house was surrounded so we went down the back stairs to the cellar. There's a cistern outside the wall. We found some shovels and dug into it—dirt never moved so fast before—before the fire got down there."

"Well, I'll be a hoptoad's granny!" Fess marveled.

"The water was neck-deep in the cistern and we had to stay there all day. I got lung fever. Jeems took me to a shanty in the woods and nursed me for weeks. Since then I've been trying to catch up with the general. Where is he?"

"Dunno, but we'll find him."

"And, Fess—"

"Yeh. What is it?"

"I met Uncle George again yesterday. He's a colonel now."

"Well, what of it?"

"His regiment was about twenty miles from here. He thought I had surrendered and I let him think so. We made more plans for after the war."

"That won't be far off now." Fess sighed. "Well, let's move along."

It was evening again when they swam their horses across the swollen Catawba River and rode into Yorkville. They learned the general was stopping at a certain house and found him alone in the garden, pacing up and down.

"Ezra!" He put both arms around him. "Ezra, boy! What a bright ending to a dark day!"

Twilight fell as Ezra told his story and the general continued pacing.

"I have given up," he said abruptly. "Mrs. Hampton is here and has persuaded me. I have sent a letter to Mr. Davis, wherever he may be. The war is over." He took another turn on the grass, vigorous still, but haggard almost beyond recognition. "Yes—over. I have not a dollar in the world, nor a place to lay my head."

"Gen'ral," Fess said, "I've got a little place up in Cashier's Valley you can allus call home."

"What a friend you are, Fess!"

"Guess I'll go look to the hosses," Fess said. "Come on, Spot."

"I will be going too," Ezra said.

"Tomorrow we will go back together and sign our paroles."

"What will that mean, sir?"

"For me, and I hope for many others, it will mean that, though we could not die for the South, we can live for her."

After a moment Ezra asked, "Do you remember, sir, the inscription you wrote in *Ivanhoe*?"

"Yes, I remember it: *Fortes fortuna juvat*—fortune favors the brave."

"The South was brave, sir, but—"

"So was the North, Ezra. They will be one again now, and surely fortune will favor it."